The anvil-jawed blackjack player j~~~~
rel of his short Colt under the security man's jaw.

Clint reached over the bar and closed his hand over the bartender's shotgun.

"Now listen, friend," Anvil Jaw said to the dealer, "if I don't get my money back in the next ten seconds I'm gonna blow this pretty boy's head clean off."

It was deadly quiet in the casino, so everyone heard Clint when he asked, "Did you lose enough to make it worth a man's life?"

The man turned his head in the direction of Clint's voice and frowned.

"Who the hell are you?" Anvil Jaw demanded.

Very slowly Clint said, "I'm the man who's going to blow *your* head off if you don't put that gun away."

"You think so?" the man asked. "You think you can kill me before I kill this here pretty boy?"

"That's not the point," Clint said. "Whether you kill him or not, you'll end up dead. Hell, it doesn't matter to me either way."

DON'T MISS THESE
ALL-ACTION WESTERN SERIES FROM
THE BERKLEY PUBLISHING GROUP

THE GUNSMITH *by J. R. Roberts*

Clint Adams was a legend among lawmen, outlaws, and ladies. They called him . . . the Gunsmith.

LONGARM *by Tabor Evans*

The popular long-running series about U.S. Deputy Marshal Long—his life, his loves, his fight for justice.

LONE STAR *by Wesley Ellis*

The blazing adventures of Jessica Starbuck and the martial arts master, Ki. Over eight million copies in print.

SLOCUM *by Jake Logan*

Today's longest-running action western. John Slocum rides a deadly trail of hot blood and cold steel.

THE GUNSMITH

132

THE GREAT RIVERBOAT RACE

J. R. ROBERTS

JOVE BOOKS, NEW YORK

THE GREAT RIVERBOAT RACE

A Jove Book / published by arrangement with
the author

PRINTING HISTORY
Jove edition / December 1992

ISBN: 0-515-10999-1

Jove Books are published by The Berkley Publishing Group,
200 Madison Avenue, New York, New York 10016.
The name "JOVE" and the "J" logo
are trademarks belonging to Jove Publications, Inc.

PRINTED IN THE UNITED STATES OF AMERICA

10 9 8 7 6 5 4 3 2 1

ONE

Clint admired the way the blackjack dealer handled the cards. He admired the way she wore her gown too. Her name was Kelly Preston, and she was the most popular dealer on *The Dead Man's Chance*. The Mississippi riverboat was owned by Clint's friend, J. P. Moses, and Moses always did have good taste in women—*and* dealers. In this case, he had combined both with great success.

Unfortunately, blackjack was not Clint Adams's game, so he wasn't playing. He was simply watching while he sipped his first beer of the night. This was his first night on the *Chance,* although not the first time he'd ever been on a riverboat. It *had* been a few years, however, and when Jack Moses had invited him to come on *The Dead Man's Chance,* he had accepted. He felt in need of some leisure time, and riding up and down the Mississippi playing poker was his idea of leisure time—especially when there was a woman like Kelly Preston aboard.

She had long red hair which she wore up, exposing a graceful neck and lovely shoulders. Her gown was emerald green, which went perfectly with her red hair and green eyes. It was also low-cut, revealing a breathless expanse of creamy cleavage. It was a wonder the blackjack players could keep their minds on their work.

1

Clint felt a hand on his shoulder, and J. P. Moses appeared next to him.

"I see you found our Kelly," Moses said.

"She's lovely."

"She is that."

"How long has she been here?"

"Only a month, and she's already increased my business at the blackjack table."

"I can see why. What about you?"

"What about me?" Moses asked.

"Well, uh, you and the lady . . ."

"The lady and I have a business relationship," Moses said. "Not that I wouldn't like to get a little more personal, but if I did I'm afraid Lily would geld me."

"Still with Lily, eh?"

"She'll be glad to see you, Clint," Moses said. "Will you be playing some poker tonight?"

"First night and all, I may just have a few drinks and scout the competition."

"Smart man," Moses said. A man across the floor was waving at them, so Moses said, "I think I'm being paged. See you later."

Clint watched Moses walk across the casino floor to handle whatever problem had come up. J. P. Moses was in complete control of *The Dead Man's Chance,* but it hadn't always been that way. J. P. Moses was an interesting story. . . .

J. P. Moses had been born in Hard Times, Louisiana, right along the Mississippi. Ever since he could remember he'd hated the Mississippi because it took the lives of his mother and father. The name his parents gave him at birth was Jean-Paul, and his father's last name was Bouchet. He had always disliked his name, though, and as if to punish his parents for dying, he changed his name to J. P. Moses as soon as he was placed in an orphanage. "J. P." were his initials, of course, and he chose "Moses" because Moses must have been the strongest man in the Bible, since he had parted the Red Sea. He always thought that Moses could probably have parted the Mississippi too . . . mud and all!

J. P. grew up in the orphanage, but he learned all about life in the streets of Hard Times and on the docks of the Mississippi. When he was fifteen he became fascinated by a riverboat gambler named Simon Chance, and whenever the gambler was in town he spent time with the young man. Chance taught him all he'd ever need to know about cards, dice . . . and women. Still, J. P. hung on to that hatred of the Mississippi, because every time a riverboat left the dock in Hard Times, Chance was on it. In the mind of the young man, the river had taken his parents, and continued to take away the man he had come to respect most in the world.

When J. P. turned sixteen he ran away from the orphanage and headed West. He wanted to get as far from the Mississippi as possible. He made his way with cards and dice, gambling in some of the toughest towns in the West: Abilene, Tombstone, and Dodge City among them. When he was nineteen he was in Abilene, where Wild Bill Hickok was marshal. Five years later, he was in Deadwood when Hickok was shot in the back and killed by the coward Jack McCall.

J. P. learned a few new things in the West, to add to his knowledge of gambling. He learned how to use a gun, and could use it quite well when the need arose. He also learned to use his fists, and could use them well when called upon. The most important thing that he learned, however, he learned in Deadwood, staring down at Hickok's body. He learned that it was foolish to hate something like a river, even the Mississippi. It was only a body of water, and to hate that was a waste of time, and time wasted was a life wasted. Hickok's life was gone, but J. P.'s was still ahead of him.

He was twenty-four years of age when Hickok was killed, and he went back to Hard Times, Louisiana, to face down the Mississippi. . . .

Jean-Paul Bouchet—or J. P. Moses, as he was now known—lived on the Mississippi now, aboard *The Dead Man's Chance*. After he had returned to Louisiana he had made it his business to learn everything he could about riverboats, and about the Mississippi. During that time he'd plied his gambling trade in the towns along the Mississippi, and on the riverboats that traveled it, until he'd had enough money saved to buy a boat of his own. He and his partner, Jason DuPree, had turned it into a floating hotel and casino.

J. P. lived on the river he had once hated. Now he rarely, if ever, left the boat or the river. In the back of his mind he could still see Hickok lying on the floor of that Deadwood saloon. That could never happen to him, not here on his boat, on *his* river— and the river *was* his now. He knew every twist and turn, and even when the Mississippi changed its course—sometimes by inches, other times by miles—he adjusted and changed with it. It was said that he could pilot a riverboat in the densest mist on the darkest night through the shallowest points on the river—which in some places was only a matter of inches in depth—and never even scrape the bottom. In point of fact he *preferred* to pilot the boat at night, and rarely did so in the daytime.

In knowledgeable circles J. P. Moses was a legend on the river he'd once hated. To most people, he was virtually unknown. Some people—customers more times than not—did not even know who he was when they boarded the boat, but they soon found out.

He was in his early thirties now, and there was only one thing J. P. Moses still wanted. Someday, somewhere along the river, he hoped to run into Simon Chance—if the man wasn't dead already.

Moses and Clint Adams had met several years earlier in New Orleans, a chance meeting during one of the few times Moses had left his boat. It was then that they'd learned how both of their lives had been affected by the death of Wild Bill Hickok. It was Hickok—whom Moses had never known, but whom Clint had known as a close friend—who formed the link that brought Moses and Clint together so that *they* became good friends.

Although they had now been friends for a few years, this was Clint's first time on *The Dead Man's Chance,* and he was impressed.

He looked over at Kelly Preston again and was *very* impressed.

TWO

"Want to come up to the wheelhouse?"

Clint turned and found J. P. Moses once again standing at his elbow.

"Or would you rather have an introduction to Kelly?" Moses asked.

"Oh," Clint said, "I think I can manage my own introduction. Let's take a look at the wheelhouse."

"Good," Moses said. "I feel like piloting for a while."

Clint looked around for someplace to put down his empty glass. In doing so he caught himself looking at Kelly Preston again. At that moment she looked up and caught him looking and smiled. He smiled back, then followed Moses from the casino.

It was a cool night, made even cooler by the breeze coming off the river.

"It's nice out here," Clint said, following Moses up some stairs.

"It's always nice out here," Moses said. "I can't believe I used to hate the river."

"It was understandable," Clint said.

Moses looked back over his shoulder at Clint and said, "Was it?"

"You were young."

"Youth," Moses said. "I guess that can forgive anything, huh?"

"Not everything," Clint said, "but a lot."

When they reached the wheelhouse Moses opened the door and allowed Clint to precede him.

"Clint, meet Jacques Bonet," he said, making the introductions. "Only the best riverboat pilot on the Mississippi."

Bonet looked as if he had been piloting riverboats for forty years. His face was seamed and leathery, and he could have been sixty—or ninety. He was small of stature, and thin, but looking at the man's hands Clint could see that there was great strength in his small frame.

"Jacques," Moses said, "this is Clint Adams, a legend in his own place, as you are in yours."

"Glad to meet you," Bonet said. He and Clint shook hands, and Clint found that he'd been right about the man's strength.

"He is tellin' the truth about me," Bonet said, studying Clint's face. "What about you?"

"As well as he knows it, I guess," Clint said with a shrug.

Bonet looked at Moses and said, "He knows you, this one, eh?"

"Take a break, Jacques," Moses said. "I'll take over for a while."

"A *little* while, eh?" Bonet said.

Moses looked at Clint and said, "He hates for anyone else to pilot her."

"You may own her," the old man said, "but she is mine, eh?"

"I know, Jacques," Moses assured the man, patting him on the shoulder. "I know."

"Excuse me," Bonet said to Clint. "I will be back shortly. Make sure he doesn't run her aground, eh?"

"I'll do my best."

Bonet left and Moses stepped up to the wheel.

"This is the only way to travel, Clint," Moses said, staring straight ahead of them. It was dark, and misty, and Clint didn't see how the man could possibly see where they were going. "I've been on trains, stagecoaches, horses, but nothing compares to this."

"What about ships?" Clint asked. "Big ones? I went to Australia once—"

"They're not like this," Moses said, interrupting him. "They're *too* big. If I were to run over something in the water here I could feel it here," he said, tapping his hands on the wheel. "That couldn't happen on one of those big ships. Being the captain of one of those would be too impersonal for me."

Clint continued to stare outside, trying to see through the mist.

"Come here," Moses said. "Take the wheel."

"Jack—"

"No, really," Moses said. "Take the wheel, Clint."

"I can't even see—"

"I'll see," Moses said. "You just hold the wheel."

"Jack, I can't—"

"Look," Moses said, releasing the wheel. It started to turn on its own, very slowly. "If you let go it starts to veer off course, slowly but surely. That's how you run aground."

"Come on, Jack—"

"Grab it, Clint, come on," Moses said, backing away from it.

"Jack—" Clint said again, but he stepped forward quickly and took hold of the wheel.

"That's good, Clint," Moses said. "Bring it back, a

little more . . . a little more . . . that's good, now hold it there. See?"

Clint actually liked the feel of the wheel in his hands. He could see what Moses meant. He could almost *feel* the water beneath them through his hands.

"Like it?"

"Yes," Clint said.

"Then give it back," Moses said, moving alongside him. "I don't want to have to fight you and the captain for her."

Clint laughed and relinquished his hold on the wheel, stepping aside.

They stood in the wheelhouse for about fifteen minutes more before Captain Bonet returned.

"I will take her back now, Boss," he said.

"Sure, Jacques," Moses said, giving up the wheel. "I want to walk Clint around her a little more anyway. See you later, eh?"

Bonet waved with one hand, keeping the other on the wheel.

They left the wheelhouse and Moses took Clint on a walking tour of the ship, until they ended up back at the casino.

"Before we go back inside, Jack, tell me something," Clint said, putting his hand on the other man's arm.

"What?"

"Why do I have the feeling there's something on your mind?"

Moses turned and looked at Clint. "Maybe it's because you're a perceptive man."

"Want to talk about it?"

Moses thought a moment, then put his hand on

Clint's arm and said, "Not tonight. Tomorrow maybe."

Clint shrugged and said, "Whenever you're ready. I'll be here a while."

"And I'm glad of it," Moses said. "Why don't you go inside and play some blackjack?"

"Blackjack's not my game," Clint said, "but I will watch some poker."

"Check out table three," Moses said. "You might find the competition there . . . interesting."

THREE

There were three poker tables, one of which was house-run with a house dealer. The other two tables were made available for private games. Table three was one of the private games.

Clint dismissed the house game immediately, and so stayed away from table one. He took the time to watch table two—perhaps for an hour—and then moved on to table three, the one Moses had suggested. After watching three hands he knew why Moses had suggested it—and it had nothing to do with the fact that there was a beautiful woman playing there, and playing well.

There were five players at the table, four men and the woman. Two of the men were just taking up space. They weren't winning, and it was plain to see why. They were being completely outplayed by the other three players, the woman and the other two men.

The woman, though a good player, was not in the class of the other two men. She appeared to be in her early thirties, with hair as black as a raven's wing that hung to her shoulders. She looked up at Clint, holding his eyes for a moment, and then looked back at her cards. Clint felt her interest in the exchanged look, and was sure that he had sent the same message.

The other two men were seated across from each other, and each recognized the other as the competition.

After Clint had been watching for an hour, one of the men looked up at him and asked, "Do you play?"

"I've been known to, yes," Clint said.

"There's an empty seat," the man said, inclining his head towards the sixth chair at the table.

"It's my first night aboard," Clint said.

"Scouting the competition first, eh?" the man said. "Interesting. You'll be playing tomorrow then?"

"Tomorrow," Clint said, nodding.

"I'll look forward to it," the man said, and gave his full attention to the game once again.

So will I, Clint thought, and moved away from the table.

Carla Dunlop was the woman seated at the poker table. When she'd seen Clint she'd become interested in him, but had not allowed the interest to take her concentration from the game. He was probably going to be on board for a while, as she would be. There'd be another time, and another place.

Clint walked to the bar and ordered a beer. In the mirror behind the bar he could see the black-jack table where Kelly Preston was dealing. It was crowded with men, both playing and watching.

There was another blackjack table with a male dealer, which had only a couple of players at it. Clint hadn't paid it much attention until he heard the raised voices. Both he and the bartender looked over that way to see what the commotion was.

"And I say you cheated," one of the players was

saying. "You been dealin' from the bottom."

"Sir," the dealer said, "please—"

"I want my money back."

"Sir, I can't do that—"

The people at the other tables were starting to watch also, including Kelly Preston and her customers.

"Tell me something," Clint said to the bartender.

"What?"

"You don't disarm men when they come on board or into the casino, do you?"

"No," the bartender said.

Clint didn't see any hip holsters, but he was sure there were guns in the place. He himself had one, the Colt New Line he wore when wearing his holster was inappropriate.

He looked around for Moses and didn't see him.

"You have security?" he asked the bartender.

"I already signaled."

Clint could see a tall, strapping young man worming his way across the room toward the commotion.

He could only see the irate blackjack player from behind, but he was a sizeable fellow and it would be interesting to see how the young man handled the situation.

"You got a shotgun under the bar?" Clint asked.

"Yep."

"Where?"

"At the other end."

"Better move it down here," Clint said, looking at the man. He tapped the bar with his finger and said, "Right under here."

The bartender, a plump, florid-faced man in his

fifties, nodded and went to get it.

"What about you?" the irate player said, addressing the other player. "Whadaya think?"

"Well," the man said, "I been losin'—"

"See?" the first man said, and the second man nodded. Clint didn't know if they knew each other, but they had obviously become allies—allies in *losing*.

The security man reached the table now and said, "What's the problem?"

The first player looked up at him and Clint saw his face in profile. The man had a jaw like an anvil, and it was tightly set.

"Your dealer has been cheatin' us . . . right?" The last was directed at the other player.

"Yeah . . . yeah, that's right," the second man said.

"We want our money back," Anvil Jaw said.

"Yeah," the second man agreed.

"Sir," the security man said, "if we could go outside and talk about this—"

"I don't want to talk about it," Anvil Jaw said. "I just want my money back."

"Sir," the security man said, and Clint saw him close his right hand around the man's upper arm. The security man was a big, tall, strong man who had probably used that move dozens of times to walk irate customers out of the casino to where they could be handled more easily and without disruption. But Clint instinctively knew that it just wasn't going to work this time.

"Let's step outside—" the security man started to say, but Anvil Jaw slid off his stool and butted the security man in the face with his head. The blood flowed from the security man's nose and mouth, and before he could react Anvil Jaw had the barrel of a short Colt jammed under the young man's jaw.

The second player was as surprised as anyone else, but recovered and fumbled his own gun from beneath his coat.

Clint reached over the bar and closed his hand on the shotgun that the bartender had moved.

"Now listen, friend," Anvil Jaw said to the dealer, "If I don't get my money back in the next ten seconds I'm gonna blow this pretty boy's head clean off."

It was deadly quiet in the casino, so everyone heard Clint when he said, "Did you lose enough to make it worth a man's life?"

FOUR

The man turned his head in the direction of Clint's voice and frowned in his direction.

"What?"

Clint hadn't yet brought the shotgun out into view.

"I asked you if you had lost enough to make it worth a man's life," Clint said. "How much did you lose anyway?"

"That ain't none of your business."

"You're disrupting my evening, friend," Clint said. "That makes it my business."

"Who the hell are you?" Anvil Jaw demanded.

Very slowly Clint said, "I'm the man who's going to blow *your* head off if you don't put that gun away."

"You think so?" the man asked. "You think you can kill me before I kill this here pretty boy?"

"That's not the point," Clint said. "That's hardly the point."

He waited a while, and then the man asked, "What *is* the point?"

"The point is that whether you kill him or not, you'll end up dead," Clint said. "Hell, it doesn't matter to me either way."

Anvil Jaw looked around, at the dealer, at the second player, at the young security man whose blood was dripping from his chin onto the floor, and then back at Clint.

"What's your interest, mister?"

"I told you, you're disrupting my evening."

"I'm just tryin' to get my money back."

"You're going about it the wrong way."

"You're gonna stop me?"

"Yes."

"You ain't even got a gun."

"I do," Clint said, "but I'm not going to use my own; I'm going to use the shotgun that's underneath this bar. That shotgun is going to splatter you all over that blackjack dealer you said was cheating you. Is that enough punishment for him?"

"Punishment?"

"That's the only thing that's going to happen to him, whether he's cheating you or not—and you won't ever see your money because you'll be dead."

Anvil Jaw seemed to think about that for a moment.

"What would *you* do?" he finally asked.

"I'd talk to his boss," Clint said. "If he *is* cheating, you'll get your money back and he'll lose his job—but first you've got to put that gun down."

Anvil Jaw didn't react immediately.

Clint looked at the other player and said, "Put your gun away, friend. You don't want any part of this."

The man hesitated.

Clint brought his hand up from below the bar and set the shotgun down on top of the bar, where everyone could see it.

"Put it away," he said again, and the second man did. "Now move away from the table. You don't want to get any blood on you."

The man hastily moved away from the table.

Clint looked at Anvil Jaw and said, "Make up your mind. Pull the trigger, or put the gun away."

Anvil Jaw stared at Clint, trying to make up his mind.

"To answer the question you asked before," Clint said, "yes, I could kill you before you killed him."

Anvil Jaw snorted and said, "How?"

"Because before you kill him, you've got to cock the hammer on your gun," Clint said, "and as soon as you do that I'll kill you before you can pull the trigger. What's it going to be, friend?"

Anvil Jaw looked around, then looked back at Clint and said, "I only wanted my money back."

"Put the gun away and talk about it."

After a few moments the man lowered the gun and the security man was able to come down off of his toes. Clint moved away from the bar, leaving the shotgun there, walked to the man, and took the gun from his hand. He looked around and saw J. P. Moses, who had entered the room at some point.

"Jack?"

Moses moved across the room to Anvil Jaw and said, "Come with me and we'll talk about it." He looked at the dealer and said, "You too."

"But Mister Moses . . ."

Moses looked around and jerked his head, and another dealer appeared to take the first dealer's place. Moses looked his thanks to Clint for defusing a potentially messy situation, and then walked out with the player and the dealer.

Clint looked at the security man and said, "You better go and get cleaned up."

The young man nodded, said, "Thanks," and walked away on shaky legs.

"Go back to your games, folks," Clint called out. "The fun's over."

Clint walked back to the bar and was aware of all the eyes that were on him. Slowly and surely, though, people turned their eyes back to their cards, or their dice, or whatever game they happened to be involved in. In the mirror he saw Kelly Preston staring at him until somebody at her table demanded some cards.

FIVE

Clint was still standing at the bar when J. P. Moses returned.

"Ed, give this man a beer on the house," he said to the bartender.

"Already did it, Boss."

Clint raised the beer in his hand to indicate that he was still working on it.

"Thanks for taking care of that situation, Clint," Moses said, "and without bloodshed too."

"Except for your security man's nose," Clint pointed out.

"That's Joe Handle," Moses said. "He's new. He was a lieutenant in the army until he decided that an army career wasn't quite for him."

"And he ends up a bouncer for you?"

"A security man," Moses said, correcting him. "He's only twenty-five, and doesn't quite know *what* he wants to do with his life."

"How many of those do you have?"

"Security men?" Moses asked. "Or Joe Handles?"

"Either."

"I've got one Joe, and five other security men. There are usually two on duty in the casino at any given time, with the third working the outside. They work in two shifts."

"You only had one here tonight."

"The other one is sick. It's lucky you were here, or somebody might have gotten killed."

"I was glad to help." Clint finished the last of his free beer and put the empty mug down on the bar.

"So what was the story?" Clint asked. Moses frowned and Clint added, "Was the dealer cheating?"

"I don't think so," Moses said, "but I can't be sure without having seen him work. I warned him, and I'll keep an eye on him."

"What about the drunk? Did you give him back his money?"

Moses gave Clint a pitying look and said, "I wouldn't be able to stay in business very long, Clint, if I gave every sore loser back his money. No, I escorted him to his cabin and told him that we'd discuss the situation further in the morning."

"And in the morning?"

"We'll be docking, and I'll have him escorted off."

"He might have more money to lose."

"There will be other suckers waiting in line on the dock to take his place."

Clint tapped the bar top with both hands and said, "I think I'll turn in."

"Did you watch some poker?" Moses asked.

"I watched," Clint said.

"Table three?"

"Interesting," Clint said. "Who's the woman?"

"I thought you'd notice her," Moses said. "Her name's Carla Dunlop. She works the Mississippi primarily, so you wouldn't have heard of her. She's sort of our version of Poker Alice."

"And the two men?"

Moses laughed and said, "I knew you'd spot them. One is Hunch Williams, and the other is Ken Dancer. Know 'em?"

"I've heard of Dancer," Clint said. Now that he knew the names, he figured Dancer was the second man, the one who *hadn't* spoken to him.

"When do you plan on playing?" Moses asked.

"I'll sit in tomorrow night."

"You mind if I watch for a while?"

"I'd rather have you sit in," Clint said. As a poker player he ranked Moses right up there with Bat Masterson and Luke Short.

Moses shook his head and said, "I don't play on my own boat, Clint."

"Maybe another time, another place," Clint said.

Moses gave him an interested look and said, "We've only played that once, right? The night we met?"

"That's right."

"Who won?" Moses asked. "Do you remember?"

Clint shook his head and said, "For the life of me I can't recall. Good night."

"Night, Clint."

Clint looked at the bartender and said, "Good night, Ed. Thanks for the loan of the shotgun."

"Anytime," Ed said.

As Clint walked away Ed leaned his elbows on the bar and said to Moses, "That is one slick hombre."

"You don't know the half of it," Moses said.

"Tell me somethin', Boss."

"What?"

"When you and him played poker that one time, who did win?"

Moses looked at Ed and said, "I really can't recall, Ed."

As his boss walked away from the bar the bartender wondered if that was the truth. Was the boss being modest in not revealing that he had won, or was he simply lying because *he* had been the one who lost?

Ed decided that he'd never know the right answer, so he might as well stop thinking about it.

SIX

As Clint stepped outside the casino onto the deck he paused to take a deep breath.

"That was a very impressive display," a woman said from the shadows.

He turned his head and was able to see only her silhouette. For a moment he thought it might be the dealer, Kelly Preston, but when the woman stepped from the shadows he saw that it was Carla Dunlop.

"Would you have killed him?" she asked.

"If I had to," he said, "but it would have been messy with the shotgun, kind of hard to do without killing somebody else—like the dealer."

"Ooh," she said, moving towards him, "that *would* have been messy, wouldn't it?"

She stopped about three feet from him. She had a shawl covering her bare shoulders and was holding it closed with one hand. She put the other hand on the railing and turned towards the water.

"I love riverboats."

"So it's not the gambling you love?"

"It's the poker," she said. "I don't play anything else, but it's also the poker *on* a riverboat. I find the combination difficult to resist."

"I guess I can understand that."

She looked at him and said, "I take it you and J. P. are friends?"

"That's right."

"That means you know who I am."

"Miss Dunlop."

"Will you be playing poker with us?"

"I will."

"Then you must call me Carla."

"All right."

"And do I get to know your name," she asked, "or will I have to wait until tomorrow and find out along with the other players?"

"Adams," he said, "Clint Adams."

"Well, Clint," she said, turning to extend her hand to him—the hand that *had* been holding the shawl closed. Now it fell open revealing her creamy cleavage. "It's a pleasure to meet you."

"The pleasure is mine," he said, accepting her hand.

"I look forward to seeing you across the table tomorrow," she said. She held his hand a moment longer, then slid hers from his grasp, gliding her nails across his skin as she did so. She took hold of the shawl and closed it once again, then turned and melted back into the shadows, presumably on her way back to her cabin.

Clint took a moment to recover his breath from the brief encounter. He wondered if she was really interested in him, or if she was just trying to set him up for tomorrow. If she could get him thinking of her as a *woman* at the poker table, instead of as an *opponent,* it would certainly work to her advantage.

He was going to have to be extra careful not to make that mistake.

SEVEN

Clint walked down to the lower deck where his cabin was located. What happened over the course of the next few minutes served to convince him that, one, he was getting old and, two, he was getting old. He was thinking too much about women—Carla Dunlop and Kelly Preston, to be precise, comparing the two in his mind—and not paying enough attention to what was going on around him. It probably also had something to do with the fact that he was on a riverboat, and not in some Western town or city where his reputation always made him a target.

He entered his cabin, wondering what would look better fanned out on his pillow, Carla's black hair or the dealer's red hair, when something hit him from behind before he had a chance to light a candle. It was a blow to the middle of his back which propelled him forward, off balance but not hurt. He banged into the chest of drawers, however, painfully hitting his left wrist, and then fell to the floor.

Because they were on a lower deck the moonlight didn't do much to illuminate the room. In the dark he saw a figure hesitate, as if trying to decide whether to move in on him or run. The decision was finally made to run, and his assailant ran out the door.

Clint got to his feet quickly, holding his wrist awkwardly, and followed the assailant out the door. On the deck he could hear footsteps running away, and had to pause for a moment to figure out which direction they were coming from, left or right. By the time he decided to go right and started running that way, he could no longer hear the footsteps. He stopped to listen, but was greeted only by silence.

The assailant had gotten away, leaving him with a painful wrist and wounded pride.

"Damn it!" he swore.

He turned and walked back to his cabin. He lit the lamp on the table by his bed and then turned the flame up. As the yellow flame bathed the room he looked around to see if anything was missing. The drawers of the chest were open, and someone had obviously gone through his clothes, but there was nothing of value in there to begin with. He carried all of his money on him rather than leaving some in the cabin. The only thing of any value in the cabin was his gun, and it was still holstered, hanging on a chair in the corner. He closed the door to his cabin and sat down on his bed to examine his wrist.

He had struck the large knobby bone, which was now tender to the touch, but he didn't think there would be any lasting damage. If the drawers hadn't been open it might not even have happened.

There was a decanter of brandy in the room and some crystal glasses, supplied for him by J. P. Moses. He poured himself a glass and drank it slowly, wondering if there was anything more behind what had happened than his walking in on a sneak thief.

He finished the brandy and decided he'd better find Moses now and tell him what had happened rather than wait until morning. The sneak thief might decide to hit another room tonight.

"That's unlikely," Moses said. "He'll probably hole up the rest of the night, and maybe even tomorrow night."

They were in Moses's cabin, which to Clint's surprise was no more impressive than his own. He had found Moses on the upper deck, and they had gone to the cabin to discuss what had happened.

"If we get real lucky," Moses went on, "he'll disembark tomorrow when we dock now that someone had seen him."

"But I *didn't* see him," Clint said.

"He doesn't know that for sure," Moses said.

"I suppose this is a pretty common occurrence around here?" Clint asked.

"We have to put up with sneak thieves just as much as hotels do, Clint," Moses explained, "but I can't help feeling that my security has let me down for the second time tonight. I think I'm going to have to have a long talk with my boys. I'm also sorry that you had to be involved for a second time. This wasn't what I had in mind when I invited you on board."

"And we still have to get to that, don't we?" Clint asked.

"To what?" Moses asked.

"What you *did* have in mind when you invited me on board."

Moses set his jaw for a moment, then said, "Look, get some sleep and join me in the dining room for breakfast in the morning at nine. We'll talk then."

"All right," Clint said. "I hope I can make it to my bed *this* time without being tossed overboard."

"Tell me something before you leave," Moses said.

"What?"

"What were you thinking about when you walked into your cabin? You don't strike me as the type who gets caught unawares very often."

Clint scowled and said, "We'll talk about that in the morning too."

EIGHT

When Clint walked into the dining room early the next morning several of the tables were occupied, but there was one in the back, hidden behind a heavy curtain, and that was where J. P. Moses was waiting for him.

As Clint moved the curtain aside and sat down Moses poured him a cup of coffee.

"Eggs?" Moses asked.

"Sure."

"With everything?"

Clint nodded.

A waiter came over and Moses told him to bring two egg breakfasts with everything.

"And another pot of coffee," Clint said.

"*Plenty* of coffee," Moses told the waiter, who nodded. "I'd forgotten how much coffee you drink."

"Some people drink a lot of whiskey," Clint said. "This won't hurt me as much."

Clint looked out through the curtain and said, "Not a lot of people having breakfast."

"Breakfast is a gambler's least favorite meal," Moses said, "especially when he's been up all night gambling."

"Want to tell me what this is about now," Clint asked, "or wait until after breakfast?"

"Might as well start now," Moses said with a shrug. "I've got a problem."

"Well," Clint said, "surprise, surprise."

"I know," Moses said, "running this kind of operation comes with built-in problems, but I've got one in addition to the usual ones."

"Like what?" Clint asked.

"There's another boat on the river offering what I offer," Moses said.

"That just sounds like good old American competition," Clint said. "Why should that worry you?"

"They're also offering whores."

"And you don't approve of that?"

"No, I don't."

"Even so," Clint said after a moment, "it still sounds like competition. They're offering what you offer, plus a little more."

"There's more."

"Like what?"

"Like sabotage."

"Oh?"

"Yes," Moses said, "and that's not playing fair, is it?"

"Well . . . maybe not . . ."

"Maybe, hell," Moses said, "that can get downright dangerous."

Clint thought a moment, then asked, "You think last night had anything to do with that?"

"A loud and bad loser, a sneak thief," Moses said. "That's nothing compared to what they might do."

"You talk like you know the people running the other boat," Clint said.

"I do," Moses said. "Cole Aldridge."

"I don't know him."

"You wouldn't," Moses said, "but I do. He's an unscrupulous businessman who up to now has stayed off the river."

"And now he's on the river."

"And there's no room for him," Moses said. "I didn't tell you why I had to hire some new security men, did I?"

"No."

"A month ago a couple of my boys were jumped on dry land and worked over by six other men."

"Six against two," Clint said, "not very good odds."

"Cole Aldridge's kind of odds," Moses said.

"How bad were they hurt?"

"I don't think either of them is up and walking yet," Moses said.

"Have you talked to Aldridge?"

"No."

"Do you intend to?"

"Day after tomorrow we'll be in Hard Times," Moses said, "and so will Aldridge. I'll talk to him there, but we've still got two days. Anything could happen."

"What do you want me to do, Jack?"

Moses was about to answer when the waiter arrived with a multitude of trays. He laid out eggs, potatoes, ham, grits, toast, biscuits, and various kinds of marmalades and jellies as well as butter. Clint and Moses took the time to fill their plates before continuing their conversation.

"As far as what I want you to do," Moses said, "I'm not trying to hire your gun or anything. I really do want you to enjoy your time on board. I just want to be able to call on you if I need you."

"Well," Clint said, "if you keep feeding me like this,

I won't be able to move if you need me . . . but I'll be here, Jack, and if there's trouble, you can count on me."

"That's what I needed to hear, Clint."

"Unless, of course, I'm in the middle of a big hand."

"Believe me," Moses said, "playing in a game with Carla, Williams, and Dancer you're going to be involved in a lot of big hands."

"Good," Clint said, "the more the better."

"You wouldn't want any advice, would you?" Moses asked. "I mean, I've played against all of them. I could tell you what to look for."

Clint shook his head and said, "I appreciate the offer, Jack, but I'll figure them out myself."

Moses smiled and said, "That's what I figured you'd say."

NINE

They docked later that morning at a town called Mudbank. Clint watched the activity on the docks from the upper deck with interest. Supplies were loaded onto *The Dead Man's Chance,* and passengers were exchanged, some on, some off. He saw Anvil Jaw getting off, with a man on either side of him. He recognized one of the men as Joe Handle, and assumed that the second man was also a member of Moses's security team.

The collection of passengers who loaded on appeared to be an uninteresting lot. At least, there were no attractive women among them, which was just as well. Clint was still thinking about Carla Dunlop and Kelly Preston, wondering which of them would be warming his bed within the next night or two. Carla certainly seemed to have the inside track, since they had spoken the night before and he had not yet even exchanged one word with the red-haired blackjack dealer. He'd also have much more contact with Carla, since they'd be playing poker at the same table.

Then again, that could work against them becoming physically involved. He *had* slept with women before with whom he had played poker, but this session had all the earmarks of being an intense one. If either he or Carla had a particularly good night, how would that affect their behavior in bed?

But he was getting ahead of himself. They hadn't even played a hand together yet.

Clint was about to move away from the rail to go in search of some more coffee when he heard a loud crack and an even louder shout, both of which were followed by a loud splash.

Back at the rail he saw that the riverboat had a winch which they used to load particularly heavy items aboard. Apparently, the wooden arm of the winch had cracked and broken, and it looked as if a crewman had ended up in the water.

Clint rushed down to the main deck, and arrived just as the man was being pulled from the water.

"My arm! Watch my arm!" the man shouted.

"What the hell happened?" J. P. Moses shouted from behind Clint. Moses came up alongside him and asked the question again, impatiently.

"I don't know, Mister Moses," the injured man said. "The winch, it just . . . snapped. I couldn't avoid it and it knocked me overboard."

"How bad is the arm?" Moses asked a man who was leaning over the injured crewman.

"I think it's busted, Boss," the man said.

"Lyle?" Moses said, referring to the injured man by name.

"It sure feels broken."

"All right," Moses said, "get Lyle to a doctor, Ross."

Ross was apparently the man who had been checking Lyle's arm.

"Right, Boss."

"Stay with him," Moses said, "and the two of you meet us in Hard Times."

"That leaves you two men light, Boss," Ross said as he helped Lyle to his feet.

"We'll make do for a couple of days," Moses said.

Ross and another man helped Lyle from the boat and into a wagon, and Ross drove the wagon away as the second man came back aboard.

"Let's look at that winch, Al," he said to the man.

"Right, Boss."

Moses and Al went to examine the broken winch, and Clint trailed along behind. He had a feeling that this incident was more than just a coincidence.

"Look here, Boss," Al said. "It splintered here where it broke—"

"So it was an accident?" Moses asked.

"—but," the man continued, "it looks like it was sawed partway through first. The first time the winch had to take some heavy weight ... snap!"

"Damn it!" Moses said. He turned and looked at Clint. "See what I mean by sabotage?"

Clint nodded.

"How was the winch when you last docked?"

Moses looked at the man he called Al, who said, "It worked fine."

"You know what that means, don't you?" Clint asked Moses.

"What?" Moses asked distractedly.

"That means that the winch was cut somewhere between there and here, by someone who was on board."

Moses looked at Clint and asked, "Are you saying it was one of my people?"

Clint hesitated before answering and looked briefly at Al.

"Al," Moses said, "find out what the hell it was we lost in the water, all right?"

"Right, Boss." If the man was insulted by being sent away he didn't show it.

"It wasn't necessarily one of your people," Clint said. "It could have been someone who boarded at your last stop, as I did, and who disembarked here . . . but only a crew member would have been able to move about the ship freely, right?"

"Damn it," Moses said again. "Aldridge has bought a member of my crew, hasn't he?"

"Who's your crew chief?" Clint asked.

"Johnny Ross," Moses said. "He just got off with Lyle, the injured man."

"How many new men do you have?"

"Not that many," Moses said. "Just the security people I had to put on."

He looked at Clint then and a stricken look came over his face.

"The new security people," he said. "I had to add them because the other ones were attacked." Moses was getting excited now. "Aldridge had my men injured so I'd have to hire new ones—*his* new ones."

"That's not necessarily so either," Clint said, still playing devil's advocate to some degree. "I mean, how could he be sure that you'd hire the people he sent? No, it's more likely that he bought one of the new people after you hired them. Of course, he could *still* have had your other men injured so that he'd *have* somebody to buy."

"Wait a minute, Clint," Moses said, "you're making my head spin. Are you saying that my new people *are* or are *not* suspect?"

"They are," Clint said. "I guess it doesn't much matter if he bought them before or after."

"Well, that's it then," Moses said.

"What is?"

"I'll fire them," Moses said. "Joe Handle and the other one, Fred . . . something."

"That might not be such a good idea."

"Why not?"

"Because if you fire them and one of them *is* in Aldridge's pocket, Aldridge can always buy somebody else. This way, we have some idea who's on his payroll."

"So we can keep an eye on them, you mean?"

"Right. Also, if it's *not* one of them, then you're firing two men for no reason—or if it is one of them, then you're firing the *other* one for no reason."

"So we keep them on and watch them."

"Right."

Moses shook his head helplessly and said, "I have to keep an eye on my own security people."

"If it is one of them, Jack, I think that one will continue to do his job. I mean, he *wants* you to keep him on, right?"

"Jesus," Moses said, shaking his head, "you know, I wouldn't mind the competition if Aldridge would just lay off the rough stuff."

Clint thought a moment and then said, "Maybe you should tell him that yourself."

"Maybe I should," Moses said. He gave Clint a look then, and Clint knew what was coming even before Moses said it.

"Would you go with me?"

"Sure I will," Clint said. "After all, it's my idea, isn't it?"

TEN

They wouldn't dock at Hard Times until the day after tomorrow, so they had until then to decide how they would approach Cole Aldridge. Clint was in favor of dealing with him head-on, but Moses was a true gambler and was wondering if there wasn't some angle they could play.

They left Mudbank behind, and Moses went off to placate the customers whose belongings the broken winch dumped into the water. They had been recovered, but Clint didn't know how much damage had been done, and frankly, he wasn't concerned. He'd let Moses worry about that.

He took a turn around the boat, and along the way ran into Al.

"Can I talk to you for a minute?" he asked.

Al, a powerfully built man in his late twenties, gave him a hard look and said, "You gonna accuse me of something?"

"Why would I do that?"

"You wouldn't talk to me in front of the boss," Al said. "That tells me you don't trust me."

"Why should I have to trust you?" Clint asked. "You don't work for me."

"I work for Mr. Moses," Al said, "and it looks to me like you and him are friends."

"Look," Clint said, "I'm not looking to make Moses think badly of anyone, but somebody on this boat cut through that winch."

"It wasn't me."

"Good," Clint said. "Then maybe you and I can figure out who it was. You willing to help me do that?"

"Sure."

"Then you'll answer a few questions?"

Grudgingly, the man said, "I guess so."

"How long have you worked for Moses?"

"A couple of years."

"Anyone else work for him that long?"

"Well, the captain longer than that, and I think Ross too."

"They're the only ones who have worked for him longer than you?"

"That's right."

"Do you think either of them could be involved with this sabotage?"

"Hell, no," Al said. "The captain loves this boat, he wouldn't do *nothin'* to hurt it."

"And Ross?"

"Ross is loyal to Mr. Moses . . . like me."

"All right," Clint said, putting his hand on one of the man's broad shoulders. "All right, Al. That means I can trust the three of you."

Al frowned and said, "You'd do that just on my say-so?"

"That, and my own instinct," Clint said. "I'm usually a pretty good judge of character, Al. What's your last name anyway?"

"Grant," the man said, "Al Grant."

"Clint Adams," Clint said, sticking his hand out.

Al took it, and could have crushed Clint's hand with his superior strength, but didn't.

"When Ross gets back on board, maybe the three of us should have a talk, huh?"

"Sure," Al said.

"Meanwhile, why don't you and I keep our eyes on the rest of the crew. Okay?"

"Okay," Al said, anxious to please now that he was trusted.

And of course Clint didn't *totally* trust anyone but himself and Moses, but it didn't hurt to have Al Grant *think* he was trusted.

"By the way," Clint asked, not because he cared but to keep his newfound friendship going, "what was it that fell overboard?"

The other man made a face and said, "Some woman's trunk."

"I hope there wasn't anything in it but clothes," Clint said. "At least they'll dry out."

"You know women," Al said. "They carry almost everything they own when they travel. Who knows what was in that trunk. We needed the winch to lift it on board, didn't we?"

"That's true enough," Clint said. "Thanks for talking to me, Al. I'll see you later."

"Sure, Mr. Adams."

"Clint."

"Okay . . . Clint."

Clint left the man where he was and went up to the casino deck. If Al Grant wasn't involved in the sabotage, then Clint had an ally. If the man *was* involved, he was probably put well off guard by Clint's talk of trust. Either way Clint had at least accomplished *something*.

• • •

A pair of eyes warily watched Clint Adams ascend from the bottom deck to the top deck, until he was out of sight. Adams was an unexpected development that Cole Aldridge was going to have to be told about—unless he was taken care of before *The Dead Man's Chance* docked at Hard Times.

Hell, who knows? That might even be worth a sizeable bonus.

ELEVEN

Clint came into the casino late that night, after the game at table three had already been going on for a couple of hours.

"They've been asking for you," J. P. Moses told him, intercepting him at the door.

"What'd you tell them about me?"

"Nothing," Moses said. "I think Carla passed the word about you, and I understand you talked with Hunch Williams last night."

"We passed a few words."

"Well, I guess those few words impressed him. You want me to walk you over?"

"Buy me a beer first," Clint said. "I won't be having any during the game, but I'll have one now."

"Make them wait, huh? All right, come on."

They walked to the bar, where Clint greeted Ed, the bartender.

"Evenin', Mister Adams," Ed said.

"I'm going to be on board a while, Ed," Clint said. "You better get used to calling me Clint."

"All right."

"Get used to not charging him for his drinks too, Ed," Moses said. "From now on everything is on the house. Got it?"

"I got it, Boss. Beer . . . Clint?"

"Just one," Clint said, "to wet my whistle."

Clint turned and looked over at Kelly Preston, the blackjack dealer, while he waited for his beer.

"Having second thoughts about not playing black-jack?" Moses asked.

"I might pass the time with a few hands," Clint said.

"She is a lovely thing, isn't she?"

"Is she . . . interested in anyone on your crew?" Clint asked.

"No," Moses said, "not even me."

"You?" Clint said. "I thought you said you were still with Lily?"

"Lily will be joining us in Hard Times," Moses said. "Besides, I was just testing the waters. Kelly seems to be all business."

"Interesting."

"Now Carla Dunlop," Moses said, "is another sto-ry."

"In what way?"

"She likes men."

"I see."

Ed set two beers on the table and both Clint and Moses turned their attention to them.

"I had a talk with your man Al," Clint said. "You trust him?"

"As much as I trust anyone on my crew," Moses said, then qualified it by adding, "With the possible exceptions of the captain and Johnny Ross. They've been with me the longest."

"Yeah," Clint said, "that's what Al told me."

"You trust him after talking to him?" Moses asked.

"I don't trust anyone but me," Clint said, "and *maybe* you."

"Thanks."

Clint looked down the bar at Ed and asked, "How long has Ed been with you?"

"A little over a year. He's probably the best bartender I ever had."

"Which means?"

"Which means he doesn't steal *too* much from me," Moses said. "He'll be okay as long as he doesn't get greedy."

"What about the rest of the crew?"

"There's a big turnover in people," Moses said. "Most of them work a few months and then move on."

"What about the dealers?"

"Same thing," Moses said. "I think Dave Plantier has been here the longest of all my dealers and croupiers, about eight months."

"Who's the newest?"

"Your lady friend, Kelly."

Clint nodded, digesting the information.

"You don't think Kelly had anything to do with it?" Moses asked.

"Like I said," Clint said, putting his mug down on the bar empty, "I don't trust anybody but you and me. Come on, walk me over to table three and make the introductions official."

Clint and Moses walked over to the poker table and waited until the hand that was in progress was over.

"Gentlemen—and lady, of course," Moses said, "this is Clint Adams. Mr. Adams would like to join your game."

"We've been waiting for you, Mr. Adams," Hunch Williams said, "ever since our meeting last night."

"Glad you could make it, Clint," said Carla Dunlop. "This game needs some new blood."

"You and Adams know each other, Carla?" Ken Dancer asked.

Carla gave Dancer a look that was designed to say nothing—and everything—and said, "We only met last night, Ken."

Dancer looked up at Clint and gave him a frank appraisal before saying, "There's a chair open, Adams. Pull it up and let's play poker."

"I'll leave you nice people to your game," Moses said. "As always, I wish you all luck."

TWELVE

The game went about as Clint would have expected. The cards weren't coming to him during the first two hours, so he spent a lot of time folding and watching the others. Actually, not having cards gave him the time not only to watch but to evaluate the other players.

Counting him there were six in all: Williams, Dancer, Carla, and two others named Arnold Leveque and Lawrence Block.

Leveque and Block were simply not very good poker players, and because of that they lost fairly constantly. They both seemed unconcerned by it, though, so Clint figured them for wealthy men who simply enjoyed playing, win or lose.

Carla was a good player, but a little reckless.

Ken Dancer knew what to do with his cards and he was ruthless when he *had* them. He was also impatient, and Clint's constant folding after three or four cards started to get on his nerves—which was fine with Clint.

The best player on the table—of the other five, of course—was Hunch Williams. He was patient, smart, and—maybe most important of all—he seemed to be very lucky. Clint wondered if Hunch was his Christian name, or if he had acquired it in his

51

youth. There was certainly no sign of hunch-playing in his poker.

"Jesus, Adams," Ken Dancer said after a bad hand for him in which he dropped a big pot to Williams, "when are you gonna do some cardplaying?"

"When I get some cards to play, Dancer."

"You got to play the cards you get, Adams," Dancer said. "You got to *make* them work for you."

"Like you just did, Ken?" Hunch Williams asked, grinning broadly. It was his deal and he was shuffling the cards.

"I played that hand perfectly, Hunch," Dancer said defensively. "Nine times out of ten that hand wins."

"Well," Williams said, "I'm glad I was here for the tenth time."

"Just deal the cards," Dancer said sourly.

As if to add to Dancer's foul mood and impatience, the cards suddenly started coming Clint's way. Dancer also realized that Carla seemed to only have eyes for Clint—besides her cards, that is. In between hands she always seemed to be looking at Clint, who didn't mind looking back. She was wearing another low-cut dress tonight, this one red. Last night's had been orange. Clint decided she liked loud, attention-getting colors—not that she *needed* the colors to get attention.

Clint had wondered when he first sat down if Carla and Dancer were involved away from the table. After the first hour he was sure of it.

"Heard we've had some excitement on board," Lawrence Block said.

"What kind of excitement?" Arnold Leveque asked.

Block and Leveque discussed what had happened with the winch and the injured crew member, and then Block said he'd heard that there was a sneak thief on board.

"That's probably a rumor," Leveque said.

"I don't know," Block said, "there's always thieves workin' these riverboats." Block looked at Carla, who was wearing a fairly expensive necklace, and said, "I hope you didn't leave too much jewelry in your room, ma'am."

Carla gave him a smile and said, "My jewelry is quite safe, thank you."

Clint took a moment to study Block for a moment. He was in his forties, with brown hair that curled up around his collar. Behind wire-frame glasses he had soft brown eyes and his stature was sort of bookish. His shoulders were rounded, and he was slender, but tall. His clothes were fairly simple, though probably more expensive than anything Clint would wear.

Leveque, on the other hand, was a stocky man in his thirties given to wearing suits with loud vests, like the red and blue checked one he was wearing tonight.

Clint wondered why Block was worried about Carla's jewelry. Could this bookish fellow have been the man he'd surprised in his cabin last night? Was he simply pumping Carla about her jewelry to try and find out if she was the kind of woman who left it in her cabin? Or had the thief disembarked at Mudbank, to look for easier pickings?

"Your play, Adams," Dancer said. "Play 'em or fold 'em."

Dancer obviously thought that Clint had been staring across the table at Carla—and indeed, Clint had probably been looking that way while his mind wandered. Letting his mind wander was not a good idea—not in a game like this.

"What is it to me?" Clint asked.

"Leveque bet fifty," Hunch Williams, the dealer, said.

Clint looked at his two hole cards and said, "I'll raise fifty."

"Finally got something worth playin', huh?" Dancer asked.

"The bet's to you," Clint said.

"Well, I'll just bump you a hundred," Dancer said arrogantly. "Let's see if you've really got somethin' you're proud of."

Carla folded, as did Lawrence Block. Williams called the bet, even though he fully expected a re-raise.

Leveque called, since he was the opener, and Clint surprised them all by just calling.

"Guess he ain't so proud of it," Dancer said.

"We've still got cards coming, Dancer," Clint said.

"If you can't bet 'em now, Adams, you might as well fold."

"Why don't I just deal and we'll find out who's got what soon enough," Williams said.

He dealt out the fourth and fifth cards, and the betting went the same way. The opener checked, Clint bet, Dancer raised, and no one raised back. Carla was openly watching Clint with curiosity. If he knew Dancer was going to raise him, why did he continue to bet into him if he wasn't going to raise back?

Williams dealt out the sixth card, the last before the final hole card was dealt.

"Check," Leveque said. The man was obviously trying desperately to improve on the cards he'd opened with, but hadn't done so or he would have bet.

Clint, who had been betting fifty and allowing Dancer to raise a hundred, said, "Bet two hundred?"

"What?" Block said. Since he was no longer involved in the game he hurriedly said, "Sorry," even though he'd voiced everyone's thoughts.

"*Now* you're tryin' to convince me you have somethin'?" Dancer asked.

Clint didn't say anything.

"Where've you been the rest of the night?" Dancer made a show of leaning over to closely study Clint's cards.

On the table in front of Dancer were four hearts, and he had been raising all along like he had two in the hole. Everyone on the table knew that he had a flush and it was at least king-high. If he had the ace in the hole, then he had a very pretty ace-high flush—unless he had an even better hidden hand.

On the table in front of Clint was a mess. All the cards were of different suits, and the highest card he had was an eight. There *was* a possibility of a straight, but that certainly wouldn't help him against Dancer's flush.

Williams and Leveque each had a pair on the table, but weren't betting like they had anything else special in the hole.

"I raise two hundred," Dancer said.

Williams, who had been playing up to then, folded and Leveque called. The man was praying, and Clint didn't think his prayers were going to be answered.

Clint purposely hesitated before he said, "Oh, I'll call."

"Ha!" Dancer said triumphantly. He beamed at everyone as Williams dealt.

"Last card coming out," the dealer said.

Clint felt Carla Dunlop's eyes on him as he examined his last card.

THIRTEEN

"Arnold?" Hunch Williams said.

"Huh?" Leveque said, looking at Williams. "Oh, I check."

"Clint?"

"Two hundred."

"Dancer?"

"Raise two hundred."

"I'll fold," Leveque said, and all eyes turned to Clint.

Since the cards hadn't been coming for Clint and he'd been chipping money in little by little for the first two hours, his stake had dwindled some. This was almost a make-or-break hand for him. It was obvious to him that he didn't have the money to stay with Leveque and Block, or even with the other players—unless he started taking some hands. As Ken Dancer said, he had to *make* things happen for himself.

"Call two hundred," he said, "and raise five."

"Five *hundred*?" Williams asked.

"Yes," Clint said, pushing the money into the center of the table, "five hundred."

"I just wanted to be clear on that," Williams said. Still the dealer, even though he was out of the hand and all the cards were dealt, he looked across the table at Ken Dancer and said, "The bet is five hundred."

"I know what the bet is," Dancer said testily. "The bastard is trying to buy the hand."

No one said anything while Dancer once again looked at his hole cards. Impatiently, then, he shoved money into the pot and said, "Call." Clint knew Dancer wanted to raise, but didn't have what it took.

Neither did he have what it took to win the hand, not if all he had was an ace-high flush.

"Four eights," Clint said, and turned over the three he had in the hole.

Dancer sat staring at the four of a kind, and then tossed his hand in on top of the money.

"I'm going out for a smoke," he said, and stood up and left.

"You crushed him," Carla said.

"He's got plenty of money," Clint said, raking in his pot.

"I don't think that's what she means," Hunch Williams said.

At that moment a waitress came over and took drink orders. Everyone ordered but Williams and Clint. She said she would bring the other man—Dancer—another drink, since he always took one when she came around.

Clint finished pulling in his winnings and then looked at the other players.

"Are all of you friends of his?"

"No," Leveque said.

"Just met him this trip," Block said.

"We play occasionally," Hunch Williams said.

Clint looked at Carla, who hesitated a moment and then said, "Not . . . *friends* exactly. If you have something to say, say it."

"I've heard of Dancer," Clint said. "He has a certain . . . reputation."

"Something some of us avoid," Williams said.

"What's your point?" Carla asked.

"After watching him play," Clint said, "I can't figure out *how* he got that reputation."

No one said anything for a few moments, and then Hunch Williams said, "I would think that you of all people, Clint, would know the answer to that."

Clint looked at Williams and said, "I, of all people, know that not all reputations are deserved. Is that what you mean?"

Williams shrugged and said, "That's as good an explanation as any."

"You're talking about his impatience," Carla said.

"Yes," Clint said. "Fundamentally he's sound, but his impatience makes him do things you wouldn't normally expect from a player of his caliber."

"He's only been like that . . . lately," Williams said.

"What do you mean by lately?" Clint asked as Leveque began to shuffle the cards.

"We played last year," Williams said, "and he wasn't like that. We played earlier this year, and I noticed the beginnings of it."

"And now?" Clint said.

"Now it seems worse than ever."

"And he must know it," Clint said.

"He does," Carla said.

"Here he comes," Block said.

"Deal, Leveque," Williams said. "Time for less talk and more poker."

Leveque dealt, including Ken Dancer in the hand.

• • •

The rest of the night Clint and Williams won steadily. Carla Dunlop won enough to come out ahead. The others—including Ken Dancer—lost. Dancer just never seemed to recover from the hand he'd lost to Clint's four eights.

"That's it for me," Block said, standing up. "I can't see anymore."

"Me neither," Leveque said. "Same time tomorrow night?"

"Sure," Williams said. "I'll be here."

"So will I," Clint said.

"See you then," Leveque said, and he and Block walked away.

Clint and Hunch Williams began to collect their money from the table. Carla Dunlop did as well, but it didn't take her as long.

Ken Dancer stood up and said to Carla, "Are you coming?"

She stood up and said, "Good night, gentlemen," and walked away.

Ken Dancer scowled and hurried to catch up to her.

"Dancer's priorities are all screwed up," Hunch Williams said. "I hate to see a good player go bad."

"It happens to everyone," Clint said, pocketing his money.

"How about a drink?" Williams said. "I believe it's on the house."

"So are my drinks," Clint said. "I think I will join you."

It wasn't unusual for big gamblers to receive free food and/or drinks from casinos, whether they were on water or land.

They walked to the bar together. Clint asked Ed

for a beer, while Williams had a whiskey.

"Helps relax me after a game," Williams said, downing the whiskey. "I notice you don't drink during the game."

"It doesn't help me concentrate," Clint said. "You don't either."

"No," Williams said. "The poker table is the one place I try to keep my wits about me at all times."

He put the empty glass down and waved Ed away when he came over with the bottle.

"What do you think of blackjack?" Williams asked.

Clint noticed that Williams was looking at Kelly Preston, who was still dealing.

"It has its appeal, I suppose," Clint said, "but I prefer longer odds than two and a half to one. It just takes too long to grind out a realistic profit."

"I know what you mean about its appeal," Williams said. "Do you play anything else?"

"Not really," Clint said. "I'm not much of a gambler—except for poker."

"Maybe I'll try a few hands of blackjack before I turn in," Williams said, "just for something to do."

Clint raised his beer mug and said, "Good luck."

They both knew that Hunch Williams had more interest in the blackjack dealer than in blackjack.

Clint watched in the mirror as Williams walked to Kelly's table and sat down alongside two other male players who were still in there pitching.

"She'll shoot him down," Ed said, "just like all the rest."

Clint didn't say anything, but inside he hoped Ed was right.

FOURTEEN

Clint was still watching Hunch Williams play blackjack—and try to engage Kelly Preston in conversation—when J. P. Moses moved in next to him. It was late, and the casino was about as slow as it would get before being closed down for the night— or morning.

"How did the game go?" Moses asked.

"I won."

"A lot?"

"I don't know that," Clint said. "I didn't count my money at the table. Let's say I've got enough reason to come back tomorrow."

"Who'd you pluck?"

"Everyone but Williams and Carla Dunlop."

"Dancer?"

Clint nodded.

"I been hearing bad things about Dancer up and down the Mississippi," Moses said. "Has his game gone as bad as I hear?"

"I'm afraid so," Clint said. "He's impatient, and he swings from impetuous to scared and back again."

"Too bad," Moses said. "He was a pretty good player, once."

"There he goes," Ed said, and both Clint and Moses looked over at the blackjack table, where Hunch

Williams was giving up on the game, the dealer, or both.

"Another one, eh?" Moses said. "Kelly sure doesn't seem to like any of our customers, Ed."

"Maybe she just likes to keep business and pleasure separate," Ed said. He looked down to the end of the bar where a pleasant-looking woman was sitting, smiling at him. "Glad I don't have that problem. Excuse me."

"What about you?" Moses asked Clint.

"What about me?"

"You ready to try some blackjack?"

"I'm beat," Clint said. "Besides, this place looks just about ready to close up."

As he said that the remaining two players at Kelly's blackjack table got up and left, and there were no longer any gamblers in the room, just dealers and croupiers.

"Stay here," Moses said.

"I want to turn in, Jack."

"Just a moment," Moses said, and walked over to Kelly. They spoke for a moment, and then she nodded and he returned to the bar.

"She's going to come over for a drink when she's finished her tally."

"A drink with you, or me?"

"Both of us," Moses said. "I told her there was someone I wanted her to meet."

"Jack," Clint said, "I'm not at my best when I'm tired."

"Just say hello, Clint," Moses said. "Don't you want to talk to all my people?"

"I'm not a detective," Clint said. "I'm not going to interrogate everyone."

"Here she comes," Moses said. "Now be nice."

Kelly came over to the bar, and Clint saw that while she was beautiful from across the room, up close she was absolutely stunning. She had green eyes and just a hint of freckles across the bridge of her nose. Her hair was not bright red, but a more subdued coppery red which suited her. She appeared to be about twenty-five.

"Kelly Preston," Moses said, "I'd like you to meet a good friend of mine, Clint Adams."

"Mr. Adams," she said, extending her hand. He shook hands with her and found that she had a grip firmer than a lot of men he'd shaken hands with. She also caught his eyes with hers and held them boldly. She knew that he had been watching her from across the room since yesterday.

"It's very nice to meet you, Miss Preston," Clint said politely.

"What kind of a night did you have, Kelly?" Moses asked.

"The usual," she said, still holding Clint's hand in hers—not that he was all that anxious to let hers go either.

"Good," Moses said. Clint assumed that "the usual" was indeed *very* good.

"I saw you playing poker tonight," Kelly said to Clint, releasing his hand. Ed came over and put a glass down in front of her. From the looks of it it was brandy, or sherry. She picked up the glass and kept talking. "Do you play blackjack?"

"Not very much," he said. "I simply don't like the odds."

"What about some of the other games?"

"No," he said, "I prefer poker."

"Why is that?"

"It's the only game where I'm not playing against the house." Even at a "house" poker table the dealer simply deals, and does not take part in the game.

"I imagine that's a very smart way to look at it," she said.

"I've always thought so," he said.

"I can see you're not like most of the men I run into," she said.

"Why do you say that?"

"Well, so many of them come to my table to play even though they either *don't* play blackjack or play it badly."

"And why do they do that?"

"To impress me, of course," she said. "Or to meet me and . . . proposition me."

"I see."

"I'm glad you're not like that," she said. Their eyes met, and the sexual tension in the air was so thick you could have sliced it with a knife.

She finished her brandy and put the glass on the bar. "I'm very tired, I think I'll go to bed. Good night, Mr. Adams."

"Good night, Miss Preston."

"Good night, Mr. Moses."

"Night, Kelly."

As she walked away Moses said, "Whew, sorry about that."

"Sorry about what?"

"The cold shoulder she gave you," Moses said. "Like to chilled my balls off."

"Really?" Clint said. "I hadn't noticed. I thought we were heating up the air pretty good."

"What?"

"Good night, Jack."

"What?" Moses said again as Clint walked away.

Clint went through the casino doors out onto the deck As he had expected, Kelly Preston was waiting there for him.

"Your cabin or mine," she said.

FIFTEEN

They went to her cabin, which, as it turned out, made no difference. It was identical to Clint's.

She had taken his hand and led him to her cabin, and when they were inside she turned and came into his arms. The first kiss was gentle, testing, their tongue tips barely touching. When the kiss was over they drew back, evaluating it, and when they both decided that they'd liked it, their mouths came together. This time there was nothing gentle about it. There was much tongue-lashing and even teeth-gnashing, which neither of them minded. When they drew apart this time there was a little blood on both their lips, and they didn't even care whose it was.

The clothes came off after that, hurriedly, *eagerly,* and then they fell to the bed together. They explored, using their hands, their mouths, their tongues, and finally he ended up between her legs, his tongue avidly working on her. She moaned, cried out, cupped his head in her hands as he worked her into a frenzy, his nose grinding into the coppery, wiry pubic hair while his tongue delved deeply into her before finding and concentrating on her straining clit. When she exploded beneath him and began to buck, it was all he could do to hold on. Finally, he slid atop her and drove the length of his penis into her in one swift move. She was so wet and slick and *hot,* and then her legs were around his hips and they were straining against each other, coming together so hard that at times their flesh slapped together audibly. He swore the bed was moving beneath them, unless it was the motion of the boat, but soon he didn't notice at all as they both settled into an eager, almost mindless rhythm that took them to the final explosion together . . .

"Why hadn't you approached me before tonight?" she asked later.

"I didn't approach you tonight," he said.

"That's right," she said, "the boss introduced us."

"And it was his idea."

"Why did you have to wait until he introduced us?" she asked. "You've been watching me for two days . . . haven't you?"

"Of course."

"Then why wait?"

"I don't know," he said. "I guess I just had the feeling you'd prefer it that way. I could see how many men approached you every day."

"Yes," she said, stretching next to him, her hands over her head, "men who can't even play blackjack. Do you know how much money it must have cost them just to be rejected by me?"

He turned his head and looked at her. The room was dark, but they were used to it by now and he could see her face. She was staring up at the ceiling, but her right hand was stroking his hip.

"Do you enjoy rejecting men?"

She looked at him now and said, "Of course. Doesn't everyone enjoy power? You know, looking the way I look—or the way *any* beautiful woman looks—gives us power over most men. We'd be fools if we didn't enjoy that power."

"I suppose."

"You have it too."

"What?"

"Power," she said, "over women."

"Oh, I don't think—"

She pinched the flesh at his waist and said, "Don't say that. Of *course* you know. You're being modest."

"And you don't have that problem?"

"Modesty?" she asked. "Oh, my, no, and you shouldn't either. Women like you, Clint, and you know it. You'd be foolish not to use that—or have you?"

He didn't answer.

"Yes, of course you have," she said. "That's why you didn't approach me. You saw *me* watching *you* and you decided to wait—which made *me* wait. Why you sonofabitch," she said, almost in awe. "You did it to me?"

He still didn't answer.

"Oh, that's wonderful," she said, rolling on top of him, surprising him.

"Whoa," he said, putting his arms around her.

"You bastard!" she said, biting his lower lip. "You gave me a dose of my own medicine."

"That doesn't bother you?"

"Bother me?" she said, looking down at him. He tasted blood and this time knew it was his, knew she had bitten through his lower lip. She knew it too, and licked the blood away. "Of course it doesn't bother me. Now I know why we were watching each other. We're two of a kind."

She kissed him then—*hard*—without giving him a chance to reply, so he replied the only other way he could. He kissed her back and began to do things to her with his hands, and she moaned . . .

"About that power," she said still later.

"It's not a *power*," he said.

"Of course it is," she said. "Look at that woman you're playing poker with."

"Carla?"

"Yes," Kelly said. "She keeps watching you across the table. Don't tell me you haven't noticed."

"Sure, I've noticed," he said, "but she watches me between hands."

"What does that mean?"

"Well, if I had this power that you say I have, she'd be watching me all the time, wouldn't she?"

"So?"

"So she's not so taken with me that she's letting it affect her game."

"Still . . . she *is* watching you." Her hand was on him again, sliding over his hip and thigh until she was stroking his semi-erect penis. "Are you watching her?"

"Of course I am," he said.

"Oooh," she said, taking him in her hand and squeezing—but not too hard. "You could have lied."

"You wouldn't have believed me," he said. "You know I like women, just as I'm sure you like men."

"But I'm particular," she said. "Do you know how many men I've rejected since I took this job?"

"No," he said, "and I don't want to know."

"Aw," she said, "how do you know just the right thing to say to a girl?"

"Come here, girl," he said, reaching for her and pulling her atop him.

"Again?" she asked, laughing, feeling him swell right there between them.

"I'm exerting my power over you . . ."

SIXTEEN

The thief forced the door on the cabin as quietly as possible and slipped inside. Of course, he had made an art of forcing doors like these, and did so easily *and* without making any noise. Once inside he waited until his eyes adjusted to the darkness. He knew that the occupant of the cabin was not inside, because he was in the woman's cabin. Actually, he would have preferred that the man and woman were in *this* cabin so he could rob the *woman's* cabin. He knew she had some nice jewelry. He just hoped that she was stupid enough to keep it in her cabin.

Once he could see in the dark he started searching the cabin for valuables. He found what must have been a second wallet—since the man obviously still had his wallet on him—with some money inside. There wasn't much, but a few hundred wasn't bad for walking-around money. He stuffed the money into his pocket and put the wallet back where he had found it. He liked to leave the cabin as he found it, so that the occupant never knew he had been there until he actually *noticed* that something was missing.

He found a ring, which looked like real gold, but he couldn't be sure in the dark. He pocketed that too.

After that he was disappointed. There was nothing else in the cabin worth taking. It wasn't a good start, but he had plenty of nights' work ahead of him and he wasn't about to become discouraged after just one.

He let himself out of the cabin, allowing the door to lock behind him. On deck he looked both ways, straightened his jacket, and then started walking. Anyone encountering him now would just think he was out for a stroll on deck.

As if to test his theory someone called, "Hey, hold it there."

His first instinct was to run, but he quelled that and turned to find himself facing a man he knew was one of the security men on board.

"What is it?" he asked.

The man peered at him, and then his face relaxed when he recognized him.

"Oh, it's you, sir. Can't sleep?"

"Uh, no, I was just out for a walk. I thought it might do me some good."

"All right, sir," the man said. "Sorry if I startled you."

"That's all right," the thief said. "It's comforting to see that the security on board is this good."

"Thank you, sir," the security man said. "We do our best."

"Good night," the thief said, and with a feeling of elation walked back to his own cabin.

The security man continued his rounds after that, secure in the knowledge that he had just done his job, even if he *had* just stopped one of the passengers.

He hoped the man wouldn't complain to Mr. Moses, though.

SEVENTEEN

When Clint entered the dining room for breakfast the next morning J. P. Moses was nowhere to be seen. He took a table in the main dining room and ordered breakfast. Kelly had already told him that she would not be up for breakfast. She usually slept late the day after she worked—especially today, she'd told him as he left her cabin in the middle of the night.

Clint was almost finished with his breakfast by the time Moses showed up. Instead of heading for his curtained table the riverboat owner joined Clint at his.

"Sleep late?" Clint asked.

"I wish," Moses said. "I was dragged from my bed by a complaining guest."

"Complaining? About what?"

"His room was broken into last night."

"Ah," Clint said, "then our sneak thief is still on board."

"Obviously."

"Who was the irate passenger?"

"Ken Dancer."

"Oh?" Clint said. "What did Mr. Dancer lose?"

"A few hundred dollars and a gold ring," Moses said. "The money didn't seem to bother him—he

77

carries most of his money on him. It's the ring he's screaming about. Apparently he attaches a lot of importance to it."

"If it was that valuable why did he leave it in his room?"

"I asked him that and he just started yelling," Moses said, shaking his head.

"Breakfast, Mr. Moses?" the waiter asked. He was the same waiter who had served them the previous morning, a white-haired man in his sixties.

"No, Angus," Moses said, "just bring another pot of coffee and a second cup."

"Yes, sir."

"And Angus?"

"Yes, sir?"

"There will be no charge for any of Mr. Adams's meals while he's on board."

"Whatever you say, sir."

As Angus walked away Clint asked, "How long has he been with you?"

"You know," Moses said, "when we talked about who had been working for me the longest I never even thought of Angus. I was thinking of crew, but Angus is more like family."

"How so?"

"He worked for my father for years," Moses said. "When I got my own boat I found him working in a hotel in New Orleans and asked him to come to work for me. He took his apron off right there and then, dropped it on the floor, and said, 'Let's go.'"

"I see."

Moses looked at Clint and said, "But Angus wouldn't be involved in this. He's even further above reproach than I am."

"Okay," Clint said, "I'm convinced."

Angus came with the fresh coffee and brought two more cups, taking Clint's used one away.

After Moses had poured two cups full Clint said, "Need I ask where Dancer was instead of his own cabin?"

"I didn't ask," Moses said, "but we'll assume that he was in Carla's cabin."

"You'd better talk to your security people and see if they saw anything during the night."

"Did *you* see anything during the night?"

"Me?"

"Sure," Moses said, "like when you were going back to your cabin from Kelly's cabin?"

"What makes you think I was in Kelly's cabin?"

"I'm not blind, Clint," Moses said. "After you left I realized what was happening between you two right before my eyes. She was waiting for you outside, wasn't she? Or did you go right to her cabin? Or was she in—"

"Never mind," Clint said. "You can draw your own conclusions. I'm too much of a gentleman to verify your assumption."

"Fine, fine," Moses said, "shut me out. I'm only the one who introduced you."

"More coffee?" Clint asked, lifting the coffeepot.

"Pour," Moses said sourly.

"What are you going to do about Dancer's complaint?" Clint asked.

"What can I do? It was impossible to calm him down. He wants me to search every cabin on the boat, and I'm not about to do that. I don't want the word spreading like wildfire that we've got a thief on board."

"He's bound to tell someone if he's that upset," Clint said.

"I managed to convince him not to."

"How did you do that?"

"I told him I'd put him off at Hard Times, and he'd never get a chance to get his money back at the poker table."

"And that convinced him?"

"It sure did," Moses said. "He seems very eager to sit down with you again. I guess you took him pretty good last night."

"There *was* one hand in particular," Clint said.

"That's what I figured. No, he'll keep his mouth shut. I told him if I hear it from *anyone* I'll just have him tossed overboard."

"That I'd like to see," Clint said. "I may just pass the word myself."

EIGHTEEN

What Moses had told Dancer had apparently done the job, because at the game that night Dancer never once mentioned what had happened. He did seem preoccupied by it, though, and it affected his play. Clint guessed that was just another sign that the man wasn't the player he once was. Clint knew that he himself was a good player, but he didn't think he could do it for a living because he didn't think he had the absolute concentration that would take.

Once again Clint was aware of the attention he was getting from Carla Dunlop, and he wondered if Carla wasn't doing it on purpose to *further* distract Dancer, neutralizing him as an effective opponent.

Block and Leveque were back again for another try, and there didn't seem to be any shortage of money. Of course, Carla and Hunch Williams were effectively playing with other people's money—as was Clint himself.

When Clint had first entered the casino he'd looked over at Kelly Preston's blackjack table. She'd graced him with a smile, but then concentrated on her work. She seemed very capable of separating her business and her pleasure, which suited Clint just fine. He preferred that to having her be the kind of woman who would be casting moon eyes his way all night.

He'd also had a short chat over a beer with Moses at the bar before sitting down to play.

"Any word on your thief?" he asked.

"No," Moses said. "My people say they didn't see anyone suspicious on deck all through the night."

"What about Dancer keeping his word?"

"I haven't heard any hint of it from anyone, so I guess he took me at *my* word."

"What about accidents? Any more today?"

"No," Moses said. "Everything seems to be as it should be, for now. Tomorrow we get into Hard Times, and you and I will go and have a talk with Aldridge. Uh, you *are* still going with me, aren't you?"

"Sure," Clint said, "I said I was."

"I'll try not to make you look like my hired gun," Moses said, "or my bodyguard."

"Don't worry about how I look, Jack, just tell him what you have to tell him."

"Right, right," Moses said. "I just hope I can keep myself from going for his throat."

"You'll do fine," Clint said. "Excuse me, I have some victims waiting."

"Good luck."

The waitress kept coming to the table to fill drink orders. All the players except Williams and Clint were drinking, and Dancer was drinking *extra* heavily. He seemed intent on losing as much money as he could. He was even outplayed several times by Leveque and Block. Midway through the night he was down what Clint guessed to be several thousand dollars, if not more. He was also very drunk and getting drunker. Clint hoped he wasn't armed, but knew that to be a false hope. Anyone who made his living playing poker was *always* armed.

"You bitch," Dancer said to Carla after she beat him out of a hand. She had bluffed him, and showed her hand so he would know it.

"Take it easy, Ken," Williams said.

"You take it easy," Dancer said sullenly. "Bitch didn't bluff you out of a hand."

"I'm sure the lady has bluffed each of us out of a hand at least once tonight," Williams said. "That's no reason to call the lady names."

"What are you," Dancer asked, "her goddamned knight in shining armor?"

Williams was the dealer and he held the cards instead of dealing them.

"Maybe you've had enough for tonight, Ken," he said. Clint didn't know if Williams was referring to poker or whiskey, but it could have been both.

"I'll tell *you* when I've had enough, Williams," Dancer said. "Just deal the goddamned cards."

Williams looked around the table. Leveque and Block averted their eyes, Carla didn't respond at all, and Clint simply shrugged.

"If the man wants to drink and play, who are we to stop him?" Clint asked.

"Well, thank you very goddamned much, Adams," Dancer said. "I don't need *you* on my side."

"Who says I'm on your side, Dancer?" Clint asked. "If you want to get drunk and throw your money at me, I'd be a fool not to do my best to catch it."

"You think so, huh?" Dancer asked. "You think you're gonna get more of my money? Deal the damned cards, Williams, and I'll show this tinhorn who's gonna get whose money."

Williams looked at Clint, who shrugged again and said, "Deal 'em."

Williams dealt, and Dancer stayed too long without the cards to back him up and lost the hand—as luck would have it—to Clint.

Leveque was gathering the cards in for his deal when Dancer's fist suddenly slammed down on the table.

"You did that on purpose!" he said, looking across the table at Williams.

The room grew quiet as the two men exchanged hot glances.

"What are you saying, Dancer?" Williams asked.

"You dealt him the winning hand on purpose."

"Are you saying I bottom-dealt that hand?" Williams asked slowly. Before Dancer could answer, Williams continued. "Because if that *is* what you're saying, Ken, then that means you're calling me a cheat. *Are* you calling me a cheat, Kenny?"

Dancer's eyes flicked around the table at the other players. Leveque and Block averted their eyes. They seemed to be very good at that. Carla just sat back and watched what was transpiring, appearing to be very relaxed.

When Dancer looked his way Clint felt compelled to say something to try and defuse the situation.

"Dancer, be realistic. Would Williams cheat and deal *himself* a losing hand?"

"Stay out of this, Clint," Williams said. "It's me he's accusing of cheating. Kenny and I will settle this between us—won't we, Kenny?"

Ken Dancer suddenly seemed very unsure of himself.

"Maybe . . ." he said, and then stopped to lick his lips, which had suddenly gone dry.

"Maybe what?" Williams asked.

"Maybe . . . m-maybe I spoke a little . . . hastily," Dancer said. His voice was very low, but everyone at the table heard him.

"You sure did," Williams said, "and maybe you've had enough for tonight, huh?"

Dancer looked at the other men at the table, but seemed incapable of looking at Carla.

"Maybe . . ." he said, and then again, "Maybe . . ." and then fell silent.

He seemed unable to say anything else, so he stood up, wiping his hands on the sides of his jacket as if they were sweaty. He started away from the table, then stopped and *did* look at Carla. He seemed to be wordlessly asking her if she was coming with him.

"I've still got a lot of poker ahead of me, Ken," she said. "Get some sleep. I'll see you tomorrow."

He nodded, ducked his head, and walked unsteadily to the door. All eyes were on him, which couldn't have made it any easier for him.

"Shall we continue to play cards?" Williams asked.

No one seemed inclined to answer, so Clint just said, "Deal 'em."

NINETEEN

Clint did very well that night, as did Hunch Williams. After Dancer left—and because of the circumstances, no doubt—Leveque and Block lost some of their concentration, so they virtually did not win a hand for the last two hours of the game. Most of the pots were won by Clint, Williams, and Carla, although Carla only took about one out of every five or six. The rest were evenly split between Clint and Williams.

When the game broke up Leveque and Block said good night and left quickly.

"They'll lick their wounds and come back tomorrow with renewed wallets," Hunch Williams said.

"If they don't get off in Hard Times," Clint said.

"Oh, that's right," Williams said. "We reach Hard Times tomorrow. Either of you getting off there?"

"No," Carla said. "I'm going all the way downriver."

"I'll be on board for a while," Clint said.

"Good," Williams said. "If Leveque and Block don't come back we'll get some new blood. Either of you care for a drink before turning in?"

"Thank you, I don't think so," Carla said. "Good night, gentlemen."

As Carla walked away Williams said, "That's a beautiful woman."

"Yes, she is."

"A drink, Clint?"

"Sure."

They walked to the bar and ordered the same as the night before, beer for Clint and whiskey for Williams.

"We appear to be rather evenly matched," Hunch Williams said.

"I don't think so," Clint said.

"No?" Williams said. "I take it you think you're a better player than I am?"

"Not at all," Clint said. "You're the better player. I've just been getting some good cards."

"You admit I'm a better player?" Williams asked, surprised.

"I'd be a fool not to admit it, Hunch," Clint said. "You do it for a living. For me it's just a hobby."

"More than a hobby."

"All right," Clint said, "more than a hobby, but less than a passion. How's that?"

"A passion," Williams said, mulling the word over. "Yeah, I guess that's what it is to me, a passion."

"So just by the nature with which we both approach the game," Clint said, "you'd have to be the better player."

"You know what I think?" Williams asked.

"What?"

Williams put his empty glass down on the bar and said, "I think I'd be glad if you don't take up poker for a living." He clapped Clint on the arm and said, "Good night."

Clint turned and watched Williams walk from the room, wondering if that wasn't the finest compliment he had ever received.

• • •

While Clint was finishing his beer J. P. Moses walked in and joined him at the bar.

"The game broke up a little earlier tonight, I see," Moses said.

"I guess so."

There were still plenty of gamblers in the room, especially at Kelly Preston's table.

Ed brought a drink over for his boss without being asked.

"What are you going to do with yourself the rest of the night, then?" Moses asked.

"I guess I'll turn in early," Clint said, looking at Kelly in the mirror. She'd be busy for hours yet.

"Not going to wait for Kelly to finish up, eh?" Moses said.

Clint looked at Moses and said, "When will we be going to see Aldridge tomorrow?"

"Just as soon as we get in would suit me fine," Moses said.

"Are you sure his boat will be there at the same time?" Clint asked.

"I'm sure," Moses said. "It's no secret where the *Chance* and his boat are at any given time."

"What's the name of his boat, by the way?"

"Huh," Moses said, shaking his head. "*The Mississippi Palace*. Can you believe that? That took a lot of imagination, didn't it?"

"I don't know," Clint said, "I think it kind of has a ring to it . . . don't you, Ed?"

Ed held both hands up in front of him and said, "No comment, gents," and walked away.

"It's got a ring, huh?" Moses said.

"Good night, Jack," Clint said. "Breakfast before we get in?"

"If you get up early enough," Moses said. "That is, if you don't wear yourself out."

"I'm going to sleep, my friend," Clint said.

"How's Kelly going to feel about that?"

"There are no strings on us, Jack," Clint said. "Just watch."

He turned and walked away from the bar towards the casino doors. As he did so Kelly looked up at him and he gave her a little wave good night. She smiled, and nodded to him.

When Clint reached the doors he turned, looked at Moses, brushed himself off as if to show that there were no strings on him, and then left.

TWENTY

When Clint reached his cabin he noticed that the door was slightly ajar. It was doubtful that the sneak thief would let himself in and then make it so obvious, but he took out his Colt New Line anyway. He didn't want any more surprises.

He pushed the door open, and as he did someone turned up the lamp on the bedside table.

"Were you expecting someone else?" Carla asked from his bed. She was holding the sheet up in front of her with one hand. Her black hair was down, tumbling past her shoulders. He wondered how far down her back it went.

"To tell you the truth," he said, "I wasn't expecting anyone."

"Then maybe you could put the gun away?"

He closed the door behind him and walked to the dresser, where he laid the gun down on top.

"What are you doing here?" he asked.

For her answer she dropped the sheet, revealing her full, rounded breasts, which were tipped with dark brown nipples.

"You mean you don't know?" she asked.

"No," he said, "what I meant was, why aren't you with Dancer?"

"After what happened tonight?" she asked. "He's probably dead drunk."

"You didn't check?"

"No," she said. "When I left the casino I came directly here."

She pointed to the dress she had been wearing all night, which lay on a chair.

"I hope you don't mind a little, um, sweat? I didn't have time to clean up."

"Neither did I," he said.

"That's all right," she said. One hand was absently rubbing one of her breasts, tracing little circles around the nipple. The gesture quickened his pulse and he felt his penis swell to bursting. She licked her lips and said, "I *like* man sweat."

Well, he thought, he *had* been comparing Kelly and Carla in his mind, hadn't he? Here was his chance to successfully compare them—in *every* possible way.

"Then it seems neither of us has a problem," he said, unbuttoning his shirt.

She laid back, putting her hands behind her neck. The movement lifted her breasts and she watched, devouring his body avidly with her eyes. When he was naked her eyes went to his erection, and seemed to lose their focus a bit.

"Um," she said, "come here."

He approached the bed and she reached out to take hold of his penis with one hand, and cup his balls with the other.

She slid off the bed, still holding him like that, and said, "Sit."

He sat on the bed and she got to her knees between his legs. With one hand still fondling his balls and the other now circling his penis at its base, she bent her head, opened her mouth, and took him inside. He gasped as her head began to bob up and down on him, faster and faster. She moaned and sighed in unison with the tempo, going, "Ohhh . . ." and "Oooh . . ." and "Ummm . . ." each time her head went up and down. At one point she slurped, as if she were a child and he was a . . . a licorice stick, or ice cream. The sound excited him even more.

He reached down to cup her hanging breasts, taking their weight in his hands, tweaking her large, hardened nipples. She braced her hands on either thigh so that she could quicken the tempo still more.

"Jesus, Carla," he said, just before he erupted into her mouth . . .

The man was asleep. His breathing was even and regular, and he didn't stir when the door opened. Neither did he move as the intruder moved towards the bed. He was obviously a very sound sleeper.

The intruder stood over the man for a moment, staring down at him until the dark was no longer a problem. With one swift movement the pillow was dragged from beneath the sleeping man's head and pressed over his face. He woke then, and found that he couldn't breathe. He started to yell, but the sound was muffled by the pillow.

The intruder leaned all his weight on one hand, holding the pillow fast, and produced a knife with the other. The knife came up, and then down, driving into the struggling man's chest. There might have been a scream, but with the pillow over his face it was hard to tell. The knife came up and down again and again, seven . . . eight . . . nine times in all, and well before the ninth time the man in the bed had stopped struggling.

The intruder released his hold on the pillow, but left it in place, even wiped the knife blade on the pillowcase before moving back to the door and slipping out.

In all the murder probably hadn't taken a full minute.

TWENTY-ONE

A comparison of the two women actually wasn't fair. Carla was by far the more uninhibited of the two, but that only meant that she was different in bed, not necessarily better.

When Clint woke the next morning Carla's scent was heavy on the bed and in the room. She had left in the middle of the night, saying that she really needed to get some sleep, and that she wasn't going to get it there with him. There was just too much else they would be doing.

Of course, the comparison that he was *going* to make was how Carla's hair and Kelly's hair looked fanned out on his pillow. Well, he still had to get Kelly into *his* bed to do that, didn't he?

He was probably a sonofabitch for bedding two different women in two nights, especially when he still had to spend several days on the boat with both of them, but he'd enjoyed both women so thoroughly that he really didn't see how he could choose.

Not without further comparison, anyway.

When Clint entered the dining room he knew something was wrong. He could feel it in the air. Moses was already there, as were Joe Handle, Al Grant, Ed the bartender, and the captain. They were gathered around a central table in the room. It wasn't hard to figure out that something was very wrong.

Moses saw Clint and beckoned him over.

"What happened now?" Clint asked.

"The worst," Moses said. "We had a killing last night."

"A killing?" Clint said. "How? Who?"

"The how was with a knife," Moses said. "The who was Hunch Williams."

"Hunch?" Clint said. "Jesus."

"He was stabbed in his bed," Moses said.

"How the hell . . ." Clint said, then realized "How" had been answered. "Who found him?"

"Al," Moses said.

"I saw that his door wasn't closed, not all the way," Al said. "I knocked, and that opened it further. I started to call out, but then I saw him on the bed with the pillow over his face. He was all covered with blood."

"Wait a minute," Clint said, "back up a minute. The pillow was over his face?"

"Someone had obviously used it to smother his cries," Moses said. "He was stabbed a hell of a lot of times, Clint. A doctor's going to have to tell us how many times once the blood is cleaned up."

"Jesus," Clint said again. "Did anyone see anything?"

"We haven't questioned anyone yet," Moses said. "We were just trying to figure out how to play this."

"You'd better figure something out quick," Clint said. "People will be coming in here pretty soon for breakfast."

"We'll be in Hard Times in an hour," Moses said.

"If we could just hold off until then we could get the law on board."

Clint thought quickly. "Well, then, put a closed sign on the door—wait a minute."

"What?"

"Why not just let them come in and have their breakfast?" Clint said. "It will keep them busy and give you time to send someone for the law."

"What about the passengers who won't want breakfast?" Moses asked. "The ones who are getting off at Hard Times?"

"Well, obviously you can't *let* them off," Clint said, "not until the law gets here."

"How do we keep them on if they want to get off?" Moses asked.

Clint thought a moment, then said, "One of two ways."

"What's that?"

"Either tell them what happened," Clint said, "or give them a free breakfast."

The free breakfast worked. There weren't many passengers willing to pass up a free breakfast, especially when it consisted of eggs, potatoes, ham, flapjacks, biscuits, *and* coffee. There *were* a few, and Moses was forced to make some sort of excuse as to why no one could leave the boat yet. He told them the gangplank was unusable. Meanwhile a crewman was lowered over the side to go for the law. By the time he returned with the police in tow there were some pretty irate people wanting to get off the boat.

Once the gangplank was in place the crewman who'd gone for the police came on board. Behind

him came a man in a suit, followed by three policemen in uniform. The man in the suit was obviously
in charge. He was in his mid-forties, with a dark
mustache streaked with gray. He was tall and well
built, with broad shoulders. Obviously a man who
kept himself fit.

"What's going on?" a male passenger demanded.
"I have to get off—"

"I'm afraid no one is allowed off this boat, sir," the
man in the suit said.

"What . . ."

The man in the suit turned to two of the policemen
and said, "Stay here by the gangplank. No one gets
off, do you understand?"

"Yes, sir," one of them said.

"Mr. Moses?" the man said, turning to J. P. Moses.

"Hello, Inspector Teal."

"I understand you have a problem aboard?"

"Yes, we sure do."

"Will you show me the way?"

"Of course," Moses said, "this way."

On the way to Hunch Williams's cabin Moses
made the introductions. "Uh, Inspector, this is Clint
Adams. He's a good friend of mine who has been
helping me with some other problems."

"I see," Teal said. "A pleasure, Mr. Adams. Mr.
Moses, are these other problems related to this one?"

Moses looked at Clint, who shrugged, and then
said, "Inspector, I'm afraid that's going to have to
be something for the police to figure out."

TWENTY-TWO

Clint followed Moses and Teal into Hunch Williams's room. The coppery smell of blood was thick in the air.

"What a mess," the inspector said.

"It sure is," Moses said.

The bed looked to Clint as if Hunch Williams had spilled every last ounce of blood he had onto it. The pillow, which was still over his face, had some streaks on it, indicating that the killer had probably wiped the knife clean on it, but other than that it was still white.

"Is this exactly the way he was found?" Inspector Teal asked.

"That's it," Moses said.

"The pillow must have been used to muffle his cries," the inspector said. "Had to have been a man to hold it down on his face like that."

"Or a strong woman," Clint said.

Teal turned and looked at Clint in surprise.

"You think a woman could have done this?" he asked, pointing at the body.

"I don't see why not," Clint said. "One hand on the pillow and the knife in the other hand."

"She'd never be able to hold him down," Teal argued.

"Sure she could," Clint said. "All she'd have to do is lean on it. After the first or second strike with the knife his struggles would have to weaken. She wouldn't even have to be that big, just lean all of her weight on it until his struggles stopped."

Teal shook his head and said, "I guess that's why I'm the professional, Mister Adams. A woman could *not* have done this."

Clint decided not to argue with the "professional."

Outside the door was the third uniformed policeman Teal had brought with him. Teal walked to the door and spoke to the man.

"Bennett, you'll stand guard on this door. Do not let anyone in or out until we make arrangements to have the body moved."

"Yes, sir."

"Mr. Moses, I'll need somewhere quiet to talk to you and your people."

"We can use the dining room, Inspector. Uh, what about the passengers who are anxious to disembark?"

"They'll have to wait," Teal said. "Please inform them all to go to their cabins and wait there until they're called for."

"Do you intend to question all of them?" Clint asked.

"Well, of course," Teal said.

"What about the passengers who have *no* intention of disembarking here?" Clint asked.

"That won't be necessary," Teal said. "It's rather obvious that the killer is someone who planned on getting off here. Nothing else makes sense."

Clint thought that the inspector was assuming a lot, but again decided to hold his tongue and let the "professional" handle the situation. It really wasn't up to him to find out who killed Hunch Williams.

"What about me?" he asked.

"What about you?" Teal replied.

"Do you want to question me?"

"Did you have any dealings with the dead man?"

"We played poker the last two nights."

"Ah," Teal said, "and who won, if I may ask?"

"We both did," Clint said.

"How could both of you have won?" the inspector asked, frowning.

"There were other players in the game, Inspector," Clint explained. *"They* lost."

"Oh, I see," Teal said, "of course. Well, I don't think I'll have any further need of you, Mister Adams. Uh, did you plan on disembarking?"

"Actually, I did," Clint said, "but I'll be coming back on board. I'm not staying in Hard Times."

"Very well," Teal said. He turned and said to Moses, "And you, sir? Of course you'll be present while I conduct my investigation?"

"Well, I *had* planned on disembarking as well. I had some business to attend to—"

"I'm afraid I'll need you here, sir," Teal said. "After all, you *are* the owner."

"Well," Moses said, giving Clint a helpless look, "if you *really* need me."

"Jack," Clint said, "I'll take care of that other matter."

"You will?"

"Sure."

Clint thought he preferred going to talk to Cole Aldridge to staying aboard while the "professional" Inspector Teal conducted his investigation.

"That's great," Moses said. "Uh, Inspector, I'll have one of my people show you to the dining room, and I'll be along shortly. I just need to confer with

Mr. Adams for a moment."

"Very well," Teal said, and then wagged a finger at Moses and added, "but don't dally, sir."

"Uh, no, I won't, uh, dally, Inspector," Moses said. Outside Hunch Williams's room Moses had Al Grant show the inspector to the dining room.

"My God," Clint said, when he and Moses were out of earshot, "that's the law in Hard Times?"

"He's quite good dealing with drunks and disorderly people," Moses said. "I think that this is a little beyond his, uh, capabilities, but what can we do? He *is* the law."

"He certainly is."

"About Aldridge, Clint," Moses said. "His boat will probably be docking within the hour, further on down the docks."

"I'll be waiting for him."

"Just *talk* to him, Clint," Moses said. "Explain that we can compete without anyone getting hurt."

"Well, of course, Jack," Clint said. "Isn't that what you were going to do? Just talk to him?"

"It *was* my intention, yes," Moses said.

"You'd better get a move on," Clint said. "You wouldn't want the inspector to think that you were dallying, would you?"

"Uh, no, I guess I wouldn't."

While Moses made his way to the upper deck, dodging irate passengers along the way, Clint made his way to the gangplank. From the second deck the inspector signaled his men to allow Clint to leave the boat, which of course set off a new uproar from the passengers who were looking to disembark.

Clint wondered if he could find a good cup of coffee in a place called Hard Times.

TWENTY-THREE

Clint managed to find a little place just off the docks that served good coffee. He knew it did because as he approached the place he could *smell* the coffee. Inside it was served to him piping hot, very black, and *very* strong.

"Too strong?" the German waiter asked him anxiously.

"There's no such thing as *too* strong when you're talking about coffee," Clint said to the man.

"*Ja,* you are right about that," the man said. "I make the best coffee on the Mississippi."

"Do you own this place?"

"*Ja,* I do, and my food is also der best."

"I'm sure it is."

"You would like something?"

"Just the coffee, thanks."

"Ah, sure," the man said. He wiped his hand on his apron and extended it to Clint with a big happy grin on his face. "My name is Bo."

"Bo?"

"*Ja.*"

"My name is Clint," Clint said, shaking the man's hand. He was a big man in his thirties, with a powerful grip.

"Did you come off *The Dead Man's Chance*? Mr. Moses' boat?"

"That's right."

"There is some excitement there, *ja*?"

"Ya—I mean, yes, there is. A man was murdered."

"*Ach,* how terrible. Will you be staying here in Hard Times?"

"No, when the boat leaves, I'll be on it."

"When will that be?"

"Probably not until the inspector finishes his investigation."

"Inspector Teal? What does he know about investigating?"

"I guess that's something we're all going to find out," Clint said.

A man and a woman came in and Bo excused himself to wait on them. That gave Clint some time alone to think, and he started thinking about Hunch Williams's murder. The way he saw it, there were three possibilities. One, Williams was killed by the sneak thief for some reason. Two, he was killed by someone working for Aldridge—which was a pretty drastic step to take just to beat out a competitor. The third possibility was that he was killed by some unknown person for some unknown reason. The chances were slim that Inspector Teal would ever figure *that* out, so maybe it *was* going to be up to Clint to do it. If they didn't find out who killed Williams, Moses might never get his boat moving again—at least not for a while. Maybe even long enough to give Aldridge the advantage he needed.

It would actually be easier if the sneak thief did it, but why would he? If he entered the room and found Williams asleep, chances are he'd just slip right out again. Why murder the man *that* way? No, being stabbed *that* many times meant that the killer had something *personal* against Williams. That let Aldridge out too. That meant that someone on board who *knew* Williams had killed him.

Suddenly, Clint remembered that Hunch Williams had virtually humiliated Ken Dancer the night before. Could Dancer have been drunk and/or angry enough to kill Hunch Williams for that?

The only way to find out the answer to that was to ask him.

Clint paid for the coffee, waved at Bo, and left the little cafe. He walked down towards the docks to board *The Dead Man's Chance* again, but that was when he saw *The Mississippi Palace.* Cole Aldridge's boat had docked, and he had promised Moses that he would talk to the man. Ken Dancer wasn't getting off the *Chance* anytime soon. He decided to keep his promise first, and then question Dancer.

From the wheelhouse of *The Mississippi Palace* Cole Aldridge had a clear view of *The Dead Man's Chance,* further down the docks. It was obvious by the crowd on board, and the curious onlookers on the docks, that *something* was going on.

"Good," Aldridge said, rubbing his hands together.

"What do you think is wrong?" Captain Caleb Thatcher asked.

"I don't know," Aldridge said, "but I hope it's something serious."

"Who is it you put on his boat anyway?" Thatcher asked.

Aldridge, a tall, good-looking man in his thirties, turned to the smaller man who was older by some ten years and said, "That's for me to know, Captain . . . and *only* me."

"Right," Thatcher said.

One of the boat's crew came up to the wheelhouse and entered.

"Sir?"

"What is it?"

"There's a man on the dock requesting to come aboard."

"Who is it?"

"He says his name is Clint Adams."

"Clint Adams?" Aldridge said, frowning. "Do I know a Clint Adams?"

"I don't know—"

"I wasn't asking you," Aldridge said. "I was asking myself. Did he say what he wanted?"

"He said he's here representing J. P. Moses," the crewman said.

"Oh, really?" Aldridge said. "How interesting."

"A hired gun?" the captain asked.

"I guess we're going to find out," Aldridge said. He turned to the crewman and said, "Find Tillis and have him meet me in the lounge."

"Yes, sir?" the man said, turning to leave.

"I'm not done yet!"

"Yes, sir?" the man said, turning back.

"After you do that let this Adams on and take him to the lounge. I'll be waiting there."

The crewman didn't move.

"Well, that's all. Go on!"

"Yes, sir."

"What are you gonna do?" the captain asked.

"I'm going to talk to the man and see what he has to say," Aldridge said. "Maybe Moses sent him over to give up. Maybe he couldn't do it in person."

"I don't think so."

"Why not?"

"I know Moses," the captain said. "He won't give up—and neither will Captain Bonet."

"That old man?"

"He's the best captain on the river."

Aldridge looked at *his* captain and said, "I hired you because I thought *you* were the best captain on the river, Thatcher. Tell me if I was wrong and I'll fire you and find someone else."

Thatcher didn't reply.

"I'll be in the lounge," Aldridge said. "See to the taking on of the new passengers."

"Aye, sir," Thatcher said.

TWENTY-FOUR

Clint followed the crewman up to the second deck of *The Mississippi Palace,* which in truth—and he admittedly had an uneducated eye when it came to riverboats—didn't look all that different from *The Dead Man's Chance.* But then, he guessed that the real difference would be in what the two boats offered to their passengers.

They came to a set of doors with the word *Lounge* above them. In the *Chance* this would have been called the dining room.

"Mr. Aldridge is inside," the crewman said, "waiting."

"Thank you."

The crewman walked away and Clint entered the lounge. Inside there was one man sitting at a table, and another man standing just behind him to his right with his hands folded in front of him.

"You're Clint Adams?" the seated man asked.

"That's right."

"I'm Cole Aldridge."

"Pleased to meet you."

"Well, I don't know if I'm pleased to meet you or not," Aldridge said.

"Why not?"

"I have to admit that although your name did sound familiar to me, I didn't know who you were until my man Tillis here told me."

"What did Mr. Tillis tell you?"

"That you're a well-known gunman," Aldridge said. "With a big reputation."

"Reputations have a way of getting big with no help at all from the people who are carrying them around."

"Well," Aldridge said, "I'd be disappointed if I believed that. Tell me, Mr. Adams, are you J. P. Moses's hired gun?"

"No," Clint said, "I'm his friend."

"Ah, I see," Aldridge said. "You see Mr. Tillis here?"

"I'd have to be blind not to see him."

Tillis lifted his chin, giving Clint an arrogant look that traveled down his nose. The man was over six feet, in his early thirties, and dressed in a gambler's dark suit, but he wasn't a gambler, of that much Clint was certain. He wore a pearl-handled Colt on his hip, and his jacket was tucked behind it to display it.

"Mr. Tillis *is* my hired gun," Aldridge said.

"How did I guess."

"So if you're here as Moses's friend and not his hired gun," Aldridge said, "you wouldn't mind giving Mr. Tillis your weapon, would you?"

Clint wasn't wearing his holster so he said, "What makes you think I'm armed?"

"Tillis?"

"He's armed, Mr. Aldridge."

"Mr. Tillis has a good eye for guns, even the hidden kind."

Clint was carrying the little Colt New Line tucked into his belt on his right hip, where he could get at it with no problem.

"So give Mr. Tillis your gun and we'll talk."

"I don't think so."

"You don't want to talk?"

"I'm not about to give him my gun," Clint said. "We can talk just like this."

"Will what you have to say take long?" Aldridge asked.

"Not at all."

"That's good, because I notice there's a lot of commotion over on the *Chance*," Aldridge said. "They probably need you over there."

"They're doing fine."

"Then say what you have to say, Mr. Adams."

"You're playing this game a little rough, Mr. Aldridge," Clint said.

"What game is that?"

"The competition game."

"Competition *is* rough, Mr. Adams."

"Not rough enough for people to get hurt," Clint said. "You and Moses can compete without *that* happening."

"Oh? Has someone been hurt?"

"You know damned well someone's been hurt," Clint said. "You've got someone on the *Chance* who's doing a lot of damage."

"Well," Aldridge said, "if I *did* have someone on that boat and I *was* paying them to do damage, I'd be glad to hear that, wouldn't I?"

"How far are you willing to go, Mr. Aldridge?" Clint asked.

Aldridge spread his hands and said, "As far as I have to, Adams. I intend to be the number-one floating casino on the Mississippi."

"Would you go far enough to murder someone?"

"Murder?" Aldridge said, frowning. "That's an ugly word. You said someone was hurt. You didn't say anything about anyone being murdered."

"Well, I'm saying it now."

If Aldridge was acting he was very good at it. He looked as if he was momentarily off guard, but he recovered quickly enough.

"That's what all the fuss is about over there?"

"That's right."

"Well," Aldridge said, putting his hands together in front of him like he was going to pray, "I guess Mr. Moses has his hands full then, doesn't he?"

"Not so full that he can't handle it."

"So then the competition will continue?"

"I'm not here to ask you to stop competing, Aldridge," Clint said, "I just don't like the *way* you compete."

"I play to win, Adams," Aldridge said. "If Moses isn't prepared to do that, then he might as well quit." Aldridge pointed at Clint and added, "You'll tell him I said that, won't you?"

"I'll tell him," Clint said.

"And will you be staying on board the *Chance* after this?"

"I'll be there."

"I could probably make room for a man of your caliber over here, on my boat. I'd pay you very well. Are you interested?"

"Not in the least."

"In that case, you'd better get off my boat before I have Mr. Tillis throw you off."

Clint looked at Tillis, who had puffed out his chest.

"Don't bother," Clint said. "He's so puffed up right

now I'd hate to have to deflate him."

"What?" Tillis said. "What did you say?"

"Forget it, Tillis," Aldridge said as Clint headed for the door. "Just forget it."

As Clint made his way off *The Mississippi Palace* he knew what Moses meant about not liking Cole Aldridge. The man seemed to be very good at making people not like him. Clint would have liked nothing better than to prove that Aldridge had something to do with the murder of Hunch Williams, but he still didn't think that was the case.

He stepped off Aldridge's boat and headed back to the *Chance* to talk with Ken Dancer.

After Clint Adams left the lounge of *The Mississippi Palace*, Cole Aldridge said, "Tillis, you told me you know who he is, right?"

"Yes, sir," Tillis said, "I know who he is. I know all about him."

"And can you take him?"

"Mr. Aldridge," Tillis said, "I can take *any*body. Believe me."

"You just may have to show me, Tillis," Aldridge said. "You just might have to do that."

TWENTY-FIVE

When Clint got back to the *Chance* there were still plenty of irate passengers on board crying out to get off. It was all the two policemen could do to keep them from storming the gangplank.

Clint boarded and pushed past the policemen and passengers, and made his way to the second deck, where he found Inspector Teal and Moses still in the dining room questioning passengers.

Clint stepped inside, but stopped right there and motioned to Moses to come over.

"Did you see Aldridge?" Moses asked in a low voice.

"Yes," Clint said, "the sonofabitch."

"Ah, you got to know him well, did you?"

"We can talk about that later," Clint said. "How are things going here?"

"Slowly," Moses said, sourly, "very slowly. At this rate—"

"I think the inspector's going about this all wrong, Jack," Clint said.

"How's that?"

He explained his thought processes, and how he had come to the decision that Ken Dancer was a good bet to be the killer.

"Maybe I should tell the inspector."

"Later," Clint said, putting a hand on Moses's arm

to stop him. "First tell me where Dancer is."

"In his cabin, I guess," Moses said.

"All right," Clint said, "you go back to the inspector and I'll go and have a look."

"Right."

"Which cabin is he in?"

"Uh—"

"Never mind," Clint said. "I'll find him."

Clint left the dining room and went outside looking for a crew member, preferably someone he knew, like Al Grant. Instead, he ran into Carla Dunlop—which was even better.

"Carla."

"Can you tell me what's happening?" she asked.

"Hunch Williams is dead. Murdered."

"What?" she said, looking shocked. "But who—what—"

"Carla, where is Dancer's cabin?"

"Dancer?" Carla said. "You don't think—"

"Williams humiliated him last night," Clint said, "and he was pretty drunk."

"Maybe *too* drunk—"

"And maybe not," Clint said. "Come on, take me to his cabin."

She hesitated a moment, then said, "Well, all right . . ."

He followed her down to the first deck and then around to the other side of the boat, away from all the commotion.

"It's here," she said, stopping in front of a door, "this one."

"All right," he said, "stand back."

Clint knocked on the door. When there was no answer he tried the doorknob and found that the door was locked. He pounded on the door again, but that still did not elicit an answer.

"What if he's dead too?"

"I hope not," he said. *That* would destroy his theory and keep them in port even longer.

"Excuse me," he said, backing up, forcing her to move aside. He braced himself against the rail and lashed out with his foot. His heel struck the door just above the knob, wood splintered, and the door flew open.

Clint took out his Colt New Line and entered cautiously. The inside of the room smelled like whiskey, and lots of it. Ken Dancer was sprawled across the bed, and for a moment Clint thought he was dead. He was about to listen for a heartbeat when the man started to snore.

"He's drunk," Clint said.

"Dead drunk," Carla said.

"Do you see him last night, Carla? After you left the casino?"

"No," she said, "I went to your room, remember?"

Clint started to look around, searching the floor for something.

"If he was this drunk," she said, "he can't have killed Williams."

"Yes, he could have," Clint said. He found what he wanted, leaned over, and picked it up. He showed it to Carla. It was an empty whiskey bottle. "I think he killed Williams, then came back here and drank this bottle of whiskey. He got dead drunk *after* he killed him."

"How did he kill him?"

"With a knife," Clint said. "Hunch was stabbed over half a dozen times."

"God!"

"Did Dancer use a knife?"

"Yes," she said, "I know he had a knife."

"Well," he said, "let's see if we can find that."

They looked around but found nothing.

"He must have been smart enough to throw it overboard afterward," Clint concluded.

"So what do we do now?" she asked.

"I'll have to wake him up and ask him if he did it," Clint said.

He went to the bed and shook the sleeping man, but he didn't move. He tried slapping his face, but that didn't work either.

"Carla, go and see if you can get me some cold towels," he said.

"Where will I get—"

"Grab a crewman and tell him what you need," he said. "Use your influence."

"What influence?"

He stared at her and said, "Your influence over men."

"Oh," she said, "that influence."

"Get moving."

"Right, right."

She left, and Clint continued to try and shake Dancer awake. After about ten minutes Carla returned with a couple of towels and a basin of water.

"Let me soak the towels," she said.

"Never mind."

Clint took the basin from her and dumped the contents onto Dancer's face. The man came alive immediately, sputtering, sitting up, his eyes wide open.

"What the hell—" he said.

"Dancer!" Clint said, grabbing the soaked man by the shoulders.

Dancer looked at him and said, "Adams! What the hell—"

"Are you awake, Dancer?"

"Of course I'm awake, damn it." He looked down at himself and said, "How the hell did I get wet?"

"Dancer," Clint said, speaking loudly and precisely, "Hunch Williams is dead. Do you know anything about that?"

"Dead?" Dancer said. "Who's dead?"

"Hunch Williams, Dancer," Clint said. "You killed him, didn't you?"

Dancer didn't answer. He seemed to be concentrating, trying to remember something.

"Dancer, answer me," Clint said. "After what happened last might in the casino, did you kill Hunch Williams?"

Dancer took a little longer and then his shoulders slumped.

"Jesus," he said. "Jesus, I did, didn't I?"

"You killed him?" Clint asked.

Dancer looked at him and said, "He made a fool out of me last night."

"Was it bad enough for you to kill him?" Clint demanded.

"I was drunk," Dancer said, "Jesus, I was drunk." He looked at Carla, who looked away. "I guess . . . I guess I didn't really mean it," Dancer said, looking at Clint.

Clint released his shoulders and stood up.

"It's a little late for that now, Dancer," Clint said. "Too damned late, in fact."

TWENTY-SIX

It was almost evening when *The Dead Man's Chance* got under way again.

After Ken Dancer had confessed to killing Hunch Williams, Clint sent Carla up to the dining room to fetch Moses and the inspector. In their presence Ken Dancer once again confessed to killing Hunch Williams, and the inspector placed him under arrest. Teal acted like he was the one who had found the killer, and Clint didn't say anything.

"You're going to let him take the credit?" Moses asked him.

"We've got other things to do, Jack, remember?"

"Right," Moses said, "you're right."

Teal and his policemen took Ken Dancer off the *Chance*, and the disembarking passengers were finally permitted to leave.

After that was taken care of no one came on board.

"Al?" Moses called. "What happened to the people waiting to get on?"

"Uh, they got tired of waiting, Boss," Al said. "They, uh, got on *The Mississippi Palace*."

"*Sonofabitch!*" Clint said. "Let's get under way before something else happens."

Moses agreed, and the *Chance* got under way and left Hard Times.

• • •

Activity in the casino was reduced due to the fact
that some people had gotten off but no one had gotten on.

"You'll pick some up at your next stop," Clint said
to Moses.

They were standing at the bar, each working on
a beer. The poker game at table three had not re-
sumed. With one player dead and one arrested it was
understandable—at least for *one* night.

Besides, Clint and Moses had things to talk about.

"You want to talk here?" Clint asked.

"Hell, no," Moses said, putting his half-finished
beer down. "Let's go out on deck."

"All right."

Moses led the way and they left the casino. Pass-
ing Kelly's table Clint realized that they had not
exchanged a word since they had made love two
nights ago. Certainly not a normal relationship.

"All right," Moses said, once they were outside,
"tell me what the sonofabitch said."

Clint related his conversation with Aldridge as
precisely as he could—in fact, almost verbatim.

"I know Tillis," Moses said then. "He has a reputation as a killer up and down the river."

"Well, as far as Aldridge is concerned, you have
your own killer."

"You mean you?" Moses said. "He thinks I hired
you for your gun?"

"That's what he thinks."

"What did you tell him?"

"I told him we were friends."

"And?"

"And that I'd be around."

"Thanks."

Clint shrugged.

"So, he didn't admit to anything?"

"No, not a thing," Clint said. "But he's behind the sabotage, all right. I could see it in his face."

"And he's not about to stop, is he?"

"I don't think so, Jack."

Moses hesitated a moment, then said, "Well, I guess we'll have to start fighting fire with fire then."

"You mean play it his way?" Clint said.

"What else can we do?"

"I don't know," Clint said, "but I sure don't want to play his game. Give me tonight and let's see if I can't come up with some wild cards to deal him."

"All right," Moses said. "You've gotten my ass out of a sling already. I might as well give you a chance to do it again."

"Did Carla stay on board?" Clint asked.

"Yes, she did," Moses said. "Why? You not satisfied with Kelly?"

"No, no," Clint said, "Kelly's fine. I mean, Carla's fine too, but—"

"Wait a minute," Moses said. "You've had *both* of them already?"

Clint didn't answer, but knew that he was looking a little sheepish.

"Jesus, are *you* looking to get killed?" Moses asked.

"Don't worry about me, Jack. Hey, did your crew chief come back on board?"

"Oh, yeah, Ross and Lyle came back on after the police left."

"Why don't we talk to them? Maybe they heard something while they were on dry land."

"Good idea," Moses said. "Come on, Lyle is in his

cabin. His arm was busted and the doc wants him
laid up for a while."

"And Ross?"

"He's back to work."

"All right," Clint said. "Lyle first, and then we'll
talk to Ross. Hey, maybe we should bring Lyle a
bottle of whiskey. That'd be a nice gesture from his
boss, wouldn't it?"

"Good idea," Moses said. "I'll go and get it. You
wait here."

While Moses went back inside for the whiskey
Clint leaned over the railing and watched the scen-
ery go by. It was mostly just trees and brush, but
every so often he'd see the outline of a shack or a
shanty.

He thought briefly about the sneak thief. Would
he have been scared off the boat at Hard Times this
time? They'd probably have to wait another night to
find out. Clint doubted that the man would strike
again, right after a murder.

The thief felt that this was the perfect night to
strike again.

No one would expect it, especially not after all
the excitement about the murder and the police on
board. All that was needed was to find a likely cabin
to hit—and the thief thought of just the right one.

TWENTY-SEVEN

Clint and Moses went to Lyle's cabin. His full name was Paul Lyle. They handed him the bottle of whiskey—for which he was grateful—and listened while he talked about his time on dry land.

"I get land-sick," he said. "I'd rather be on a riverboat than anywhere else."

Moses said he knew how he felt.

Clint said he'd rather be on horseback, which made him think of his big black gelding, Duke. The horse was back in Labyrinth, Texas, being looked after by his friend Rick Hartman.

Lyle explained that he'd heard nothing about Cole Aldridge or *The Mississippi Palace* while he was on dry land. Clint and Moses decided to leave the man alone. His face was drawn and pale, and it was obvious that his broken arm was causing him some pain. Hopefully, the whiskey would act as a pain-reliever to some degree.

After talking with Lyle they went and found Johnny Ross. He echoed what Lyle said about not hearing anything about Aldridge or his boat. They didn't press the man and allowed him to go back to work. They went back to the casino.

• • •

Since table three was available Clint and Moses took their beers from the bar to the table. Moses didn't maintain a table in the casino as he did in the dining room. The casino was for gambling, not sitting around drinking or eating.

"A little head-to-head?" Moses asked, producing a deck of cards.

"A dollar a hand," Clint said. "Five-card stud."

"There's no adventure in that," Moses said, dealing the first two cards. "The cards speak for themselves. There's no skill involved."

"Maybe I should go and play blackjack," Clint said, looking past Moses.

They each put a dollar on the table and Moses dealt the rest of the cards. Moses took the hand with a pair of nines.

"See?" Moses said. "You had four hearts on the table. If we were betting you could have bluffed me."

"*I* could have bluffed *you?*"

"Sure you could," Moses said. "Anyone can bluff anyone if they have the nerve."

"I'm sure," Clint said. "All right, we'll play dollar-limit, just for fun, okay?"

"Okay."

This time Clint dealt, and when an ace fell in front of Moses he bet a dollar. Clint called. He dealt the third card, and Moses had a pair of aces. A king fell in front of Clint, matching the one he had in the hole.

"A dollar," Moses said.

"Call."

Clint dealt the fourth card. Moses got a three, while Clint got another king. He now had three kings, which certainly beat two aces, but what if Moses had an ace in the hole?

"A dollar," Moses said. "See? This isn't working either."

"Why not?"

"Because normally I'd bet heavy here, to get you out so you don't improve on the kings. Just betting a dollar doesn't do anything."

"I call," Clint said. "Remember, it's just a friendly game."

"Poker is never a friendly game," Moses said.

Clint hesitated before dealing the last card.

"What's wrong?" Moses asked.

"I don't think I want to deal this last card," Clint said.

"Why not?"

"Because of what you just said," Clint said. "You're going to be mad when I beat you."

"When *you* beat *me?*" Moses asked. "You think you can beat me in this hand?"

"Sure."

"Deal the card," Moses said.

"This is the last hand, Jack," Clint said. "I'm not playing with you anymore after this."

"Sore loser."

"We'll see who loses."

The fifth cards fell and, on the surface, did not improve either of their hands. Moses had bought an eight, and Clint a five.

"A dollar," Moses said.

Clint had a feeling that he was going to win, and if he was playing in a real game he would have gone with that feeling and raised.

Ah, what the hell . . .

"Raise a dollar," Clint said.

"Now you're talking," Moses said. "I raise a dollar."

"Call."

"No nerve," Moses said, turning his hole card over.

He had aces and eights. He had turned the card over without even realizing what he was doing, and now realized that this was the famed "Dead Man's Hand" that Hickok had been holding when he was killed.

Clint turned his hole card over to show three kings.

"You're beat," he said. He stood up, leaving the money on the table.

"Where are you going?" Moses asked.

"To play some blackjack," Clint said, "just for fun."

"What about the money?"

"Give it to Ed," Clint said. He wanted to get away from the table with those cards spread out on it, those aces and eights. When Hickok was killed, shot in the back by a coward, it had been the worst thing that had ever happened to Clint up to that point in his life. He'd lost a good friend, and been haunted for years after that by the bullet that would one day catch *him* that way. Recently, he *had* been shot in the back and had survived. At the time he'd thought that had purged him of the ghost of the bullet, but apparently it still remained. . . .

After Clint walked away Moses sat there staring at the offending cards. Hastily, he gathered them up and mixed them in with the rest of the deck. He'd been there when Hickok had been shot. That coincidence—him being there when Clint's friend was shot—had been the tie that had bound him and Clint in friendship. When he'd seen that his hand had developed into aces and eights he should have folded, but he'd been too competitive, too intent on beating Clint for a pot of a few dollar bills.

He didn't play poker very much himself anymore, not since he had taken to running the *Chance*. He guessed he should either give it up completely, or go back to it.

TWENTY-EIGHT

When Clint sat down at Kelly's table there was only one other player there, a man who seemed more intent on her than on the game. It was as if he was just pushing money across the table at her.

"New player?" she said to Clint, as if he were a stranger who had just sat down.

"I'll play a few hands," Clint said.

"I gotta warn you, friend," the man next to him said. "She's tough."

"Maybe she wouldn't be so tough if you paid attention to your cards," Clint said.

Instead of taking offense as he might have, the man simply said, "Believe me, it won't help."

Clint saw what he meant. He played five hands and lost them all, including two hands where she drew twenty to beat his nineteen, and twenty-one to beat his twenty.

"That's it for me," the other man said. He tossed Kelly his last ten-dollar chip and said, "See you tomorrow, Kelly."

"Good night, Sam."

As the man walked away Clint said, "You know him?"

"I know all my players," she said, tucking her tip away. "In fact, I know most of them better than I know you, and I haven't slept with any of them."

"I'm sorry we haven't had a chance to talk since the other night," he said.

"Do you want to keep playing, or should I pack it in?" she asked.

"No," he said, "you've convinced me even more that blackjack is not my game."

They continued to talk while she packed up her table.

"I understand things have been happening," Kelly said.

"How much do you know?"

She shrugged. "Hunch Williams was killed. Ken Dancer was arrested for it. That seems to have broken up your poker game."

"It'll pick up again," he said. "There are always new players."

"Well, Carla Dunlop is still aboard," Kelly said. "I saw her earlier this evening. I'm sure she'd love to still play with you."

He wondered if there was a double meaning in that statement somewhere. Did she know that he had spent one night with *her* and the next night with Carla? He didn't think so.

"We'll probably get started again tomorrow," he said.

"So how much do you know?" Kelly asked. "More than me, I bet. You and the boss seem pretty close."

"We're friends," was all Clint would say.

"Are you here to help out?"

"I'll help if I can."

"Things have been happening around here," she said. "I mean, other than murder. Talk has it that we and the *Palace* are in a war."

"There's some competition going on, yeah," he said.

"Competition?"

"Well, maybe it's turning into a little more."

She stopped cleaning up and looked directly at him.

"You know, I've heard of you, Clint."

"Have you?"

"I know reputations can be deceiving, and I already know you well enough to know that some of the things I've heard aren't true."

"But?"

"You're not here because you were hired, are you?" she asked.

"Why are you asking?"

"Just out of curiosity."

"I told you before," Clint said, "Moses and I are friends. Besides, I *don't* hire out."

She noticed the edge in his voice and immediately looked sorry.

"I apologize," Clint said. "Here comes your boss. I'll let you and him settle up for the night."

"Clint."

"I'll just get one more beer before I turn in," he said, and headed for the bar.

At the bar he stared into his beer, shaking his head at himself. In the span of half an hour he'd allowed himself to become annoyed at both J. P. Moses and Kelly Preston. Maybe he was getting thin-skinned in his old age.

Or maybe he was just annoyed at himself. He didn't know which was the case. He just knew that he had to forget about it. He had to be on this boat for a few more days at least, because he had promised

Moses he'd help out, and he always kept his prom-
ises. There was no point in causing tension to form
between him and *anyone*—least of all a friend, or a
beautiful woman.

TWENTY-NINE

Standing alone at the bar, nursing his beer, Clint suddenly came up with an idea. He turned to watch Moses finishing up with his dealers and croupiers, then waved him over. By the time Moses reached the bar Ed had a beer there for his boss. Clint noticed that Kelly had already left while he was moping in his beer.

"Clint, I'm sorry about before . . . at the table . . ." Moses said.

"Never mind," Clint said. "I've got an idea."

"About what?"

"About how you can resolve this competition between you and Aldridge, between *The Dead Man's Chance* and *The Mississippi Palace*."

"How?"

"Which is a better boat?"

"Well, the *Chance,* of course," Moses said. "That is, unless you ask Aldridge that question."

"Challenge him to a race."

"What?"

"A race," Clint said. "From one part of the Mississippi to another. Say, from Mudbank to Hard Times, and back again. What's that, a two-day trip?"

"If we take our time, yeah," Moses said. "But what will this prove?"

"Is Aldridge a gambler?"

"Well, of course," Moses said. "Who else but a gambler would own a gambling boat?"

"Then offer it to him as an all-or-nothing proposition," Clint said.

"All or nothing?"

"Right," Clint said. "The winner gets the Mississippi all to himself. The loser leaves."

Moses rubbed his jaw, thinking it over.

"You *can* beat him, can't you?" Clint said.

"I have the best boat," Moses said, "and the best captain. Of course I can beat him."

"Then what's the problem?"

"There *is* no problem," Moses said. "I'll do it."

"Good."

"But what if he loses, and doesn't abide by the results?"

"Challenge him in public," Clint said. "Make it as public as possible so that if he loses and *doesn't* abide by the result, he'll be branded a welsher."

Moses thought it over quickly and then smiled.

"I like it," he said. "I like it a lot. It appeals to the gambler in me."

"Let's hope it appeals to the gambler in Aldridge," Clint said.

They stood in silence for a while, working on their beers, and then Ed came over.

"Can I say something, Boss?"

"Sure, Ed, go ahead," Moses said.

"I couldn't help hearing what you were talking about," the bartender said, "and I was just wondering . . . what happens if you lose? I mean, what happens to all of us?" By "all of us" he meant the people who worked on *The Dead Man's Chance*.

Moses looked at Clint and said, "He has a point."

"Don't think about losing," Clint said.

"Not for me," Moses said. "It never occurred to me that we might lose, but I do have to think about the people who work for me. I've got a responsibility to them."

Clint shrugged. He really had nothing to say on the subject. That was up to Moses.

The gambler looked at the bartender and said, "What do you think I should do, Ed?"

"If it was up to me?" Ed said. "I'd go ahead and race the bastard—but if I was you, Boss, I guess I'd let everybody know what I was planning, and see how *they* felt about it."

Moses digested that for a moment, then nodded and said, "You're right. Ed, you call a meeting. At this time tomorrow night I want everybody who works on this boat—and I mean everybody—in here for a meeting. I'll put it to them and see what they think."

"Sounds good, Boss," Ed said. "I'll take care of it."

As Ed walked away Clint said, "And if they don't want you to do it?"

"They'll go along with me," Moses said. "I'm sure of it."

"Then why have the meeting?"

"To give them the *chance* to speak against the idea, even though I don't think they will."

"Well," Clint said, "when and how you do this is up to you. I'm going to turn in."

"Kelly went to her cabin," Moses said.

Clint just waved and walked away from the bar, Outside on the deck he took a deep breath. It was easy for him to tell Moses to put everything he owned on the line—everything he had and everything his employees had too. Clint wondered if the people who worked for Moses would really go along with this.

If they did, that would be the biggest show of loyalty he had ever seen.

THIRTY

The next day went by uneventfully. There were no accidents and no murders. During the course of the day Clint saw Carla and also Arnold Leveque, who had not disembarked at Hard Times as Lawrence Block had. They agreed to meet once again at table three that night to try to put the game together again. Clint doubted they'd have any trouble coming up with one or two other players.

During the course of the day Clint met some of the other passengers, and there was one in particular he found interesting. The man said he had not come on board to gamble, but to simply ride the river and prepare himself to start a book he was planning to write. They talked while standing up on the third deck, near the wheelhouse.

"I'm going to call it *Life on the Mississippi*," the man said. "I have been all over the world, but I always end up coming back to the river."

"Have you been a writer for very long?" Clint asked.

"Oh yes, a long time," the man replied.

"What's your name?"

"My name," the man said, "is Samuel L. Clemens, but I do much of my writing as Mark Twain."

"By God," Clint said, "I've read your newspaper articles in San Francisco, and in the New York

Herald and *Tribune*. I've also read your *Innocents Abroad*. It was brilliant."

"I am flattered, and pleased that you enjoy my work," Twain said. He had a mighty head of hair and a large mustache that obscured his upper lip. He was in his early fifties, and his once-dark hair was turning white. At the present time each color was fighting for dominance.

They spoke further, and when Clint finally introduced himself Twain was amazed.

"The Gunsmith, you say?" he replied. "I've read those godawful penny dreadfuls about you. My God, they can't all be true, can they?"

"Of course not."

"No, of course not," Twain said. "Now that I've met you I can see that. Tell me, Mr. Adams."

"Clint, please."

"I would be pleased if you would call me Sam."

It was then that Clint realized that this man actually *was* Samuel Clemens, and not Mark Twain, just as he was Clint Adams and *not* the Gunsmith.

"Then I hope you'll call me Clint."

"Clint then," Clemens said, "I know there's been some excitement on board, but I know very little about it. Would you be able to, uh, enlighten me?"

"You're not going to write about it, are you?" Clint asked.

"Well," Clemens said, "not immediately."

"Actually," Clint said, "it might be better if you did."

"Would you care to explain?"

Clint, excited now, said, "I'd like very much to explain, Sam. Let's find someplace where we can sit down."

• • •

Clemens was very excited.

"Steam races are a very big thing on the Mississippi, Clint," he said.

"Would you be willing to cover it?" Clint asked. "With you writing it up Aldridge would have to agree, and would then *have* to abide by the results."

Clemens thought a moment, then said, "By God, yes, I believe I will. It's pure luck that I'm here during a winner-take-all event such as this. Tell me, what will be the route? New Orleans to St. Louis is a twelve-hundred-mile run. That would certainly test both boats. Why, I remember back in '70 when the *Robert E. Lee* made the Orleans to Cairo run. They made it in three days and one hour."

"Well, Sam," Clint said, "to tell you the truth, we were thinking of something a bit shorter than that."

"Well, there's Louisville to Cincinnati. That's— what is it?—about a hundred forty miles. With a full head of steam they could make that in ten hours."

"How far is it from Hard Times to Mudbank?" Clint asked.

"Hard Times to Mudbank?" Clemens asked, obviously disappointed—but then he brightened. "Wait a minute. I think that's about two hundred and twenty miles, isn't it? Wait a minute. In '70 the *Robert E. Lee* went from New Orleans to Natchez—that was about two hundred and seventy miles—and they made it in just over seventeen hours."

"New Orleans to Natchez?" Clint asked.

"We'll be in New Orleans in two days, won't we?" Clemens asked.

"As a matter of fact," Clint said, "we will."

"Well," Clemens said, spreading his arms, "that's

perfect. Along the way we can stop and I can file a story with a local paper. The other papers will pick it up off the wire."

"Especially with your name on it," Clint said.

"Modesty prevented me from pointing that out," Clemens said. "Is this a finished deal, Clint?"

"No," Clint said, "not until Moses has a meeting with his crew tonight, but once you issue the challenge to Aldridge in print, that'll be it."

"Will Mr. Moses agree?" Clemens asked. He had said earlier that he'd heard of Moses, but that he had to this point kept his identity to himself so as not to attract too much attention while he was formulating his book.

"Sam," Clint said, "I think once he hears that you're involved, he'll insist. Do we have you for this then?"

Clemens extended his hand to Clint, and as Clint grasped it said, "Done!"

THIRTY-ONE

"Samuel *Clemens?*" J. P. Moses asked.

"Yes."

"Mark *Twain?*"

"That's right."

"Here on my boat?"

"Yes."

"Why didn't he let me know?"

"He was keeping to himself."

"What made him talk to you?"

Clint shrugged and said, "I'm an interesting guy."

"And he's willing to help us?"

"He'll announce the race in the papers, and then he'll cover it," Clint said.

"What papers?"

"Local," Clint said. "He'll give the story to a local paper, but when the others see his name on it they'll pick it up."

"Aldridge will *have* to accept the challenge."

"Or be ruined."

"And he'll *have* to keep his word if he loses."

"Or be ridiculed."

They were in the dining room, having dinner, and had just finished their steaks when Clint told Moses all about Sam Clemens.

"Why didn't you tell me this earlier, when we sat down?"

"I didn't want you to choke," Clint said.

"Well, where is he? Why didn't you invite him to have dinner with us?"

"I did," Clint said. "It seems he's been having his meals sent to his room, and he didn't want to change that tonight. He's in his room now, working."

"Writing," Moses said.

"Yes."

"Sam *Clemens* on my boat."

"Right."

"Mark *Twain!*"

"Will you stop saying that?" Clint said.

"Can I tell the others tonight?"

"Of course."

"They're sure to go along with me now."

"That's what I figured."

"We'll have to notify Mudbank *and* Hard Times about the race."

"Uh, not Mudbank."

"What?"

"And not Hard Times."

"What do you mean?"

"Well, come on, Jack," Clint said. "You couldn't expect Sam Clemens—I mean Mark *Twain*—to be interested in a *little* race."

"A little race?"

"So we expanded a bit on the distance."

"Expanded?" Moses asked. "How much?"

"New Orleans to Natchez."

Moses moved his lips soundlessly while doing some mental figuring, then looked at Clint and said, "That's two hundred and seventy miles if it's an inch."

"Right."

"Do you know how long that would take us?"

"It took the *Robert E. Lee* a little over seventeen hours back in '70."

"The *Chance* is not the *Robert E. Lee,* Clint," Moses said. "She's not built for that kind of—"

"You won't be racing the *Robert E. Lee* either," Clint said, interrupting him, "just *The Mississippi Palace.*"

"Yes, but—"

"Come on, Jack," Clint said, "you *said* your boat could beat her."

"Well, yeah, but I was thinking of—"

"And this might even be better," Clint said. "I mean, if the *Chance* isn't built for speed, she'll have time to *build* speed this way."

"I mean," Moses said, "I wanted to get this over with quickly."

"It'll be quick," Clint said. "I mean, say, twenty hours? Is that too much to ask?"

"A race of this distance will get a lot of attention," Moses said. "The people at both ends will want to be involved, they'll want to promote the damned thing, like a prize fight."

"Promote?"

"Clint, you don't think we're just going to line up, say ready, set, go, and that's the end of it?"

"Um . . . why not?"

"It'll be weeks before we can get this thing set up," Moses said.

"Weeks?"

"And you said you'd stay until it was resolved," Moses reminded him.

"Yeah, but . . . weeks?"

"Well, maybe we can get it set up in a week to ten days."

"Ten *days*?"

"Hey," Moses said, "this was *your* idea, remember?"

Clint nodded weakly, saying, "Yeah, my idea . . ."

"And a damned good one, I might add," Moses said. "It's just going to take . . . a little longer than either one of us figured."

THIRTY-TWO

Since no new passengers got on at Hard Times, they couldn't find any new players for the game at table three. The others seemed to be either too intimidated—or too scared.

"You know what it is?" Carla said at one point to both Clint and Leveque.

"What?" Leveque asked. They were playing three-handed until they could find another player, and Leveque was taking the worst of it.

"They're afraid."

"Of what?" Leveque asked.

"Of this game," she said. "After all that happened to Hunch and Dancer."

"One's dead, and the other killed him," Leveque said.

"I see what you mean," Clint said.

After a moment Leveque said, "Oh, yeah, me too."

"They think this game is . . . jinxed," she said.

"That's silly," Clint said.

"Well, I didn't say *I* thought it," she said, "but there are others who probably do."

"What would you do if you heard of a game that was jinxed?" Clint asked.

She thought a moment, then smiled and said, "I'd play in it. That'd be a *big* gamble, wouldn't it?"

"You're right," Clint said, "it would."

Clint went up to the bar and spoke briefly to Ed, then came back.

"What did you tell the bartender?" Carla asked.

"To pass the word that this game is jinxed."

Within half an hour they had another player. An hour later they were joined by another, and they had a game.

When the last of the gamblers left the casino the members of the crew started to file in. Eventually there was no one in the room who didn't work on the boat, except for Clint. Even Paul Lyle, with his arm in a sling, was present, as was Captain Bonet.

When Clint saw the captain he sidled over to Moses and said, "Jack, I don't think it's a good idea if *everyone* is in here."

"I know," Moses said, patting Clint's arm. "I've got a man in the wheelhouse, and another out on deck."

"Sorry," Clint said.

"Don't worry about it," Moses said. "It just means we're both on our toes."

"All right, settle down, everybody," Johnny Ross yelled. "The Boss has something he wants to say."

Clint wondered if Moses had already gone through it with his crew chief.

It took a while, but everyone finally fell silent and looked at Moses.

"I have an announcement to make," he said. "Well, actually it's not an announcement, it's more like a proposal. I want you all to listen, and then I want to hear what you all think about it."

He went on to explain about the proposed race,

about what it would mean if they won—or lost—
and then told them about Mark Twain and the news-
papers.

"Now I know a lot of you will be thinking about
your jobs if we lose, and I'll understand if you're
against this. I don't expect you all to feel the way
that I do—"

"Boss?" Johnny Ross said, interrupting him.

"Yes, John?"

Ross took a few steps forward, separating himself
from the rest of the crew.

"Boss, when you mentioned this to me today, I
started talking with the members of the crew, and
I had *them* talk to others." He looked over the crew
and asked, "Is there anyone here who didn't hear
about this already?"

No one replied.

"I see," Moses said.

"So we all talked about it, and we came up with
a decision, and I've been picked to give you our
answer."

"All right, John," Moses said. "What's the answer."

Ross hesitated then said, "Boss . . . let's run *The
Mississippi Palace* right into the ground!"

The crew erupted then, cheering and surging forward to pat Moses on the back and give him their
support.

Clint turned to Ed, who was still behind the bar,
and said, "Let me have a beer so I can drink to
loyalty."

After the last of the crew filed out—after they all
had a celebratory drink—Ed asked, "Anything else,
Boss?"

"Just draw two more beers, Ed, and then you can go. I'll close up."

"Sure."

Ed put two beers on the bar and said good night.

"Some crew, huh?" Moses asked.

"All but one," Clint said.

"Yeah," Moses said, "we still have Aldridge's man to consider."

"Or woman."

"You think it's a woman?"

"I'm just saying it's possible," Clint said.

"When can I talk to Mr. Twain?" Moses asked.

"Tomorrow," Clint said. "I'll set it up for tomorrow morning."

"Good," Moses said. He raised his mug and said, "Well, at least the sneak thief seems to be gone, huh?"

"Yep."

At that moment Al Grant came in and said, "Boss?"

"Yeah, Al?"

"While we were all in here listening to you?"

"Yeah."

"Someone broke into our cabins, Boss," Al said. "Some goddamned thief stole our stuff!"

THIRTY-THREE

As it turned out only five of the crew's rooms were broken into, and what they lost really didn't amount to that much, but it still angered Moses that it had been done. He felt responsible.

"There's no need for you to feel blame," Clint said.

"They were listening to me," Moses said. "I was keeping them busy while some thief went through their rooms. I'm telling you, Clint, if I find out who it is—"

"If we're lucky," Clint said, "the thief and Aldridge's agent will be one and the same, and we can close them both down."

"Yeah," Moses said, "but first we have to find them."

"I know," Clint said, "but not tonight. Let's turn in. In the morning we'll talk to Twain. We'll end this, Jack. I promise you we'll end it."

Moses nodded.

"I have to talk to my people, Clint, and then I'll go to bed," he said. "You go on."

"All right," Clint said. "I'll see you in the morning."

On the way back to his cabin Clint decided to stop by Kelly's. He knocked on the door, then knocked again when there was no answer. She was either sleeping soundly already, or off somewhere with some of the other crew members, probably discussing the upcoming events.

He stopped at Carla's room next, but she didn't answer his knock either.

He wondered if the order in which he'd gone to their cabins unconsciously indicated his preference.

In the morning Clint and Moses met with Twain in his cabin. The three of them went over what Twain would write—of course, with Twain composing it. All they did was make certain that *what* he said was what they wanted said. *How* he said it was up to him.

The next step was to stop someplace that had a newspaper, no matter how small.

"It's not one of our stops," Moses said, "but I know Bayou Blue has a paper."

"Bayou Blue?" Clint asked.

"It's just a small town really, but it's got a paper and a telegraph. It's just not one of our usual stops."

"When can we stop there?" Twain asked.

"Probably within the hour."

"Good," Twain said. "By the time we reach New Orleans you may have Cole Aldridge's answer waiting for you there."

"I hope so," Moses said, "and I hope he'll say yes."

"He'll say yes," Twain said, a twinkle in his eye. "When he reads this, he'll say yes."

Moses clapped his hands together and then rubbed them eagerly.

When they stopped at Bayou Blue they created a stir, both on board and off. Several of the passengers wanted to know why they were stopping, and of course the people of the town wondered as well.

"They'll all know soon enough," Moses said to Clint.

"If they can read," Clint said.

"Do you think the editor will run it?" Moses asked.

"Jack," Clint said, pointing to the man going down the gangplank with Al Grant, "that's Mark Twain, not some penny-dreadful novelist. The editor will jump at the chance."

"Yeah, yeah," Moses said, "you're right, of course. What newspaperman wouldn't want a story by Mark Twain in his paper?"

"Right."

Clint turned to walk away from the third deck rail, but Moses grabbed his arm.

"Do you think you should have gone with him, Clint?" he asked.

"Why? He only needed someone to show him where the newspaper office was," Clint said, "not body-guard him. He's not in any danger, Moses. After all, Aldridge can't know that we've stopped here."

"Yeah," Moses said, "but we announced to the crew last night what we were doing, and if Cole's—what did you call it—agent is a member of my crew . . ."

Clint turned back to the rail and looked down at the gangplank.

"All right," he said, "I don't think anything's going to happen, but I'll go after Mr. Clemens just to be on the safe side." He turned to Moses and added, "But don't let anyone leave this boat, Jack."

"I won't," Moses said, "but that don't mean some-body hasn't already left . . . somehow."

"Yeah," Clint said sourly, "right. Spies have a sneaky way about them, don't they?"

"Yeah," Moses said just as sourly, "like sneak thieves."

As Clint hurried down the gangplank Moses's last words echoed in his head. He hoped that by recruiting Sam Clemens into their plan that they—he—hadn't put the man's welfare—or life—in danger.

THIRTY-FOUR

Of course Clint did not get directions to the newspaper office from Moses, so by the time he found the place Clemens and Al Grant were coming out.

"Clint," Clemens said. "What are you doing here?"

"I just wanted to make sure you got back safely," Clint said.

"You think I'm in some kind of danger?" Clemens asked.

"It's possible," Clint said. "With everything that's been happening we just didn't want to take any chances." Clint looked at Al and said, "This is not to slight you, Al. You came along as a guide. Now you know there might be trouble. Let's keep our eyes open. All right?"

"Sure, Clint," Al said. If the man's feelings had been hurt, he was easily appeased.

"How did the editor of the"—Clint looked at the sign on the window—"*Bayou Gazette* take it?"

Al laughed before Clemens could reply.

"Clint, I thought the man was gonna fall on his knees," Al said, shaking his head.

"Needless to say," Clemens said, "he will run my article."

"When?" Clint asked.

"Today," Clemens said. "By tonight it will be on the wire, and by tomorrow—well, who knows."

"And tomorrow night we'll be in New Orleans."

Clemens nodded.

"If Aldridge is any kind of a man he'll wire his reply to New Orleans," Clemens said, "and you'll just have to wait for him to get there."

"I hope he reads it," Al said.

"Oh, he'll read it," Clemens said. "Someone is bound to show it to him."

Sooner than they might have expected Cole Aldridge saw the article in a copy of an even smaller newspaper than the *Bayou Gazette*. *The Mississippi Palace* had to pull into the small dock of a small town to pick up some needed supplies. A member of the crew picked up a newspaper while he was on dry land, and brought it back to Aldridge to read.

"By God," Aldridge said.

"What is it?" Tillis asked.

They were seated at a table in the lounge, having coffee while waiting for the supplies to be loaded.

"Moses has outdone himself this time," Aldridge said, handing the newspaper to Tillis.

Tillis took it and laboriously read it. Reading was not his strong point.

"Mark Twain?" he said. "Don't I know that name?"

"You should," Aldridge said, "but I'm surprised if you do."

"What's all this mean?" Tillis asked. " 'The Spirit of the *Robert E. Lee*' and all that stuff?"

"Twain is a smart man," Aldridge said. "He's painted me into a corner by invoking the name of one of the Mississippi's most famous steamboats."

"And what's that mean?"

"It means that Moses thinks he's gotten his way this time," Aldridge said, "but *I* think he's bitten off more than he can chew this time."

"Are you gonna race him?"

"Oh, yeah," Aldridge said, "we'll race."

"What if he beats you?"

"He won't," Aldridge said. "Don't forget we have an ace in the hole."

"Ace in the—oh, you mean—"

"Yes, I mean . . ." Aldridge said. Of course he meant that his agent aboard the ship would make sure that *something* went wrong right at a crucial moment. Of that he was sure.

He turned to leave and Tillis said, "Where are ya going?"

"To tell the captain to turn this tub around," Aldridge said. "First we'll wire New Orleans with our reply, and then we'll be on our way there." Aldridge stopped at the door, looked at Tillis, and said, "I don't know how they got him on their side, but I hope I get to meet Mark Twain."

When they got back to the *Chance* Sam Clemens went back to his cabin, Al went back to work, and Clint found Moses sitting at his table in the dining room, having lunch.

"Back already?" he said. "Is it done?"

"It's done," Clint said.

"Well, get Mr. Twain so he can eat lunch with us," Moses said. "We have to celebrate."

"He said he had work to do," Clint said, sitting across from Moses.

Angus the waiter came over and Clint ordered lunch.

"This is going to work, Clint," Moses said. "I can feel it. Cole won't be able to resist."

"And once he accepts," Clint said, "the rest will be up to you."

"No," Moses said, "it will be up to her."

"Who?"

Moses made an all-encompassing gesture with both hands and said, "Her."

"Oh," Clint said, realizing that he meant the boat, "*that* her."

They finished their lunch and had Angus bring another pot of coffee.

"Jack?"

"Yes?"

"When's the last time you asked this boat to go faster than a crawl?"

Moses thought a moment, then said, "Never. I've never been in that much of a hurry to get up or down the river."

"Never?"

Moses shook his head. "Never."

"She runs on steam, right?"

"Right."

"So we don't know how she'll react to being all stoked up and asked to go, you know, fast?"

"She'll be all right, Clint," Moses said. "This boat is put together."

Clint sincerely hoped that she was put together well enough *not* to fall apart at a crucial moment.

Then again, a steam engine didn't fall apart when it was abused . . . it exploded.

THIRTY-FIVE

By the time they reached New Orleans the word had spread. The city fathers turned out and their arrival was met with a festival atmosphere. It was as if Mardi Gras had come early.

"Jesus," Moses said, looking down at the crowd.

"We can probably forget about our sneak thief," Clint said. "He can get off here and disappear with no problem."

"Will he want to?"

"You're racing after this," Clint said. "I sort of assumed you'd want to do that with as few people aboard as possible."

"That's right," Moses said. "Only the essential crew will come along."

"Well," Clint said, "that leaves the thief out—and me as well."

"No," Moses said. "This was your idea. I want you in on the end."

"I appreciate that, Jack," Clint said, "if you don't think my weight will hold you back."

"Nah," Moses said, "we'll just throw a couple of tables overboard."

Clint looked down at the crowded dock and the crowded lower deck and then said, "I guess you'd better go down and talk to those people."

159

"They're going to want to promote the hell out of this thing," Moses said.

"See if you can get them to do it quickly, will you?" Clint asked.

"I'll do my best."

As it turned out the editor of the *New Orleans Examiner* was on the dock, and had in his pocket the telegraph message from Cole Aldridge. When Moses came off the boat the editor pushed his way to the front of the crowd and held the reply out to him. Moses took it, read it, then turned, looked up at Clint, and held it up over his head with one hand while pointing to it with the other.

Clint saw the gesture and knew what it meant.

The race was on.

The best Moses could do was get the waiting time down to a week. That would give New Orleans and Natchez time to gear up for the race. The distance was officially given as 268 miles. The *Robert E. Lee* had done it in seventeen hours and eleven minutes.

The Mississippi Palace arrived in New Orleans two days later, in the evening. By that time passengers and crew were off the *Chance,* except for Moses's security men, who were keeping an eye on the boat in the hopes that they could keep it from being sabotaged by some of Aldridge's people.

The biggest hotel in the city, the New Orleans House, made rooms available for the crew. Clint and Moses got their own rooms, as did Mark Twain, while the rest of the crew had to double and triple up. Still, it was a hotel that crew members might otherwise have not stayed in.

Another hotel in town, the State House Hotel, made rooms available for the crew of *The Mississippi Palace*.

The captains of both ships remained on board.

Four days before the race was to start the principals involved—J. P. Moses and his captain, and Cole Aldridge and his captain—met in the dining room of the New Orleans House to iron out the details. Clint decided not to join them, and remained in the hotel bar until Moses came in to join him. The riverboat owner stopped at the bar for a beer and carried it over to Clint's table.

"Is it all set?" Clint asked.

"Yes," Moses said. "In four days. We'll start off at five in the evening."

"Evening? Why not the morning?"

"Haven't you learned anything?" Moses said. "It's customary for riverboats to leave port between four and five in the evening."

"I guess I never really paid attention to what time it was when we left some port," Clint said. "How will the race work?"

"We'll start off side by side," Moses said, "and see what happens."

"Can this be done without any stops?"

"That depends," Moses said. "I'm going to try and arrange for a thirty-cord woodboat to hook up alongside us. That should carry us through."

"A woodboat?"

Moses explained that they would load a "woodboat" with thirty cords of wood to be used to keep the steam at the level they needed.

"Doesn't that add weight?"

"It does," Moses said, "but without it we'd have to stop someplace along the way to load up. This way there are no stops, and once we unload the boat and cut it loose we'll *really* move."

"What about Aldridge's boat?"

"I don't know how he's going to work it," Moses said.

"What's the most important part of this, Jack?" Clint said. "I mean, what is it that's going to make us beat them and not them beat us? Is it the boat?"

"Nope," Moses said, "it's the pilot."

"The pilot?"

"The captain," Moses said. "The best pilot will win the race, Clint."

"And who's got the best pilot?"

"We do," Moses said without hesitation, "and Aldridge knows it. Bonet's the best in the business right now."

"And who does Aldridge have?"

"His pilot's name is Caleb Thatcher," Moses said.

"Do you know anything about him?"

"I know him," Moses said. "He's a good man, a good pilot, but he can't match Bonet's knowledge of the river. Bonet's been up and down this river for thirty years."

"Excuse me if this sounds ignorant," Clint said, "but I've heard that the Mississippi can actually change course from day to day."

"That's true."

"Then even though Bonet's been on it for thirty years, it could change on him right in the middle of the race."

"If it does," Moses said, "he'll handle it, don't worry."

"Well, then, if we know and Aldridge knows that we have the best pilot, that means he's got to try something," Clint said.

"What can he try?" Moses asked. "There won't be any passengers on board, and I'll just keep the crew I know I can trust—and he *can't* sabotage the boat beforehand, because then there won't be any race."

"Still . . ."

"Still nothing," Moses said. "He's either going to have to beat us fair and square, or pull something *during* the race."

"Like what?"

"That," Moses said, "we're just going to have to wait and see."

Clint frowned into his beer.

"What is it?" Moses asked.

"Nothing."

"Come on," Moses said. "Are you starting to worry about this?"

"Well," Clint said, "it *was* my idea, and if you lose . . ."

"Whoa, wait a minute," Moses said. "Sure it was your idea, but it was a damned good one—and you didn't talk me into anything. I decided to go ahead and do it—and my *crew* supported that decision. This is out of your hands, Clint, so don't go worrying or feeling guilty about it. I mean, even if we *do* lose, it won't be your fault."

"Fine," Clint said. "I'll just keep telling myself that."

THIRTY-SIX

Later that night Clint found himself in his room, in bed with Kelly Preston. It had happened quite by chance. He had stayed in the bar for hours after Moses left, and when he came out into the hotel lobby there she was—and he wanted to *stop* thinking about the race.

When she saw him a look came over her face, and he just took her hand and led her upstairs. It *could* have been Carla Dunlop. At that moment he just wanted a woman, someone to occupy his time, and his mind, and Kelly Preston certainly filled that bill.

They proceeded to occupy each other for the better part of the night.

On the morning of the race Clint woke and stared down at Kelly Preston. More than once he had wondered if she was the one working for Aldridge, but some of the sabotage that had been done *had* to have been physically handled by a man. Of course, it was possible that Aldridge had *two* people on the *Chance,* but he chose now to believe that Kelly was just what she appeared to be—a blackjack dealer and a beautiful woman who was wonderful in bed.

He woke her by working his tongue around her nipples until she reached up to wrap her fingers in his hair. They stayed that way for a while until she slid her hands down over his back and was reaching for his buttocks.

"Come here, come here . . ." she cooed.

He moved atop her and she grabbed his buttocks and pulled on him until he slid inside of her.

"Oooh, yeah . . ." she said in his ear.

He slid his hands beneath her to cup *her* buttocks, and he started moving in her in long, deep strokes. She made a moaning sound deep in her throat and wrapped her legs around his hips, jerking her hips in tempo with his . . .

"Today's the day," she said. She was lying on her side, supporting her head with her right hand, watching him get dressed.

"Yep."

"You're going along?" she asked.

"Jack asked me to."

"You want to."

He looked at her and said, "You're right. I want to see this through to the end."

"Be careful, Clint."

He found the tone of her voice odd and paused to look at her.

"Why do you say that?"

"Both sides have a lot riding on this race," she said. "I just don't want anything to happen to you. You will be careful, won't you?"

"I'm always careful, Kelly," he said. He reached for his holster and strapped it on. He hadn't been wearing it on the streets of New Orleans, but today was different. He was going to have it on during the race, *and* while he and Moses were going over the *Chance* from stem to stern.

"Where are you going?" she asked.

"Breakfast with Jack first," he said, "and then he and I are going over the boat."

"You think someone did something to it already?"

"He's had two men on the boat since we arrived in New Orleans," Clint said. "There's no chance anyone could have gotten on board."

"Unless it was the two of them," she added.

"He and I are going to check it anyway," Clint said. "Before we start that race we want to make damned sure the boat is in top shape."

He started for the door and she said, "Hey, come here."

He walked over to the bed and she snaked one arm around his neck and gave him a long, deep, wet kiss that would have gone on forever if he had let it—and he wanted to!

"I'll be there to see you off," she said.

"I'll be looking for you," he answered, and left the room.

THIRTY-SEVEN

Clint Adams and J. P. Moses stood on the third deck of *The Dead Man's Chance*, just outside the wheelhouse, and looked down at the boat. They had just finished a process which had taken hours, and were convinced that no part of the *Chance* had been sabotaged.

"You still look worried," Moses said to Clint.

"I am," Clint said. "From what I've learned and seen of Cole Aldridge, I can't believe that he's going to play fair during this race."

"Well, maybe he won't," Moses said. "Maybe it's *during* the race that he'll try something. We'll just have to be extra alert for it."

"I wish we *had* found something so that we could fix it," Clint said.

Moses put his hand on Clint's shoulder.

"Forget it, Clint," Moses said. "Now all we have to worry about is the race itself."

Suddenly, something occurred to Clint. "Wait a minute."

"What?"

"That isn't all we have to worry about."

"What do you mean?"

"Where's Bonet?"

"He's back at the hotel," Moses said. "I told him

to get some rest while you and I were checking the boat."

"So other than right now, he's been on the boat the whole time?"

"That's right."

"Come on!" Clint said.

"What's wrong."

"Jack, this is the only chance Aldridge will have to get at Bonet before the race," Clint explained as they hurried from the boat. "Didn't you tell me it would come down to who had the best pilot?"

"That's right," Moses said, with a sinking feeling in the pit of his stomach, "I did."

Jacques Bonet was not comfortable in J. P. Moses's hotel room. He was *never* comfortable unless he was on *The Dead Man's Chance*. That was his home, his *life*. He couldn't wait until Adams and Moses were finished with the boat and he could go back aboard. He should have insisted on staying aboard even while they were checking the boat, but Moses had been insistent himself.

He was sitting on the bed, fully clothed, waiting for Moses to return. When he heard the scratching at the door he assumed it was Moses trying to fit his key into the lock, so he got up and opened it.

"It's about—"

Clint and Moses ran from the docks onto the streets of New Orleans and hurried to the New Orleans House. As they approached it Clint saw two of Moses's men on the front porch.

"Get them around to the back," he shouted at Moses, "and meet me upstairs."

He left Moses there talking to his men and ran through the lobby, ignoring the stares he was attracting. When he reached the second floor he saw that his timing had been perfect. If he had thought of it a moment later, he would have been *too* late.

There in the hall, outside of Moses's room, Jacques Bonet was struggling with two men. The bandy-legged little pilot was giving them a hell of a tussle, and Clint joined the fray.

He left his gun in his holster and grabbed one of the men by the shoulder. He turned him around and smashed him on the jaw with his right fist. The man staggered back and fell to the floor, taking with him a small table that crumbled beneath his weight.

"Hee-hee," Clint heard Bonet cackling. The second man had turned to look at Clint, and Bonet swung his fist and struck the man in the face. The blow had little effect, but the older man seemed to be enjoying himself.

The second man pushed Bonet away from him and turned to face Clint. He was bigger than Clint and when he swung his big right arm Clint ducked under it, stepped inside, and hit the man in the stomach twice. The big man grunted, but only staggered back a few steps.

By this time the first man had gotten to his feet and was moving in from Clint's other side. Before he could do anything, however, Jacques Bonet shouted and launched himself at the man. The little captain caught the man around the waist and used all of his inconsiderable weight to pull him to the floor again.

The second man charged Clint, who sidestepped

and put his hands on the man's back to add force
to his lunge. The man continued on and struck the
wall. A crack worked its way up towards the ceiling,
and Clint knew that *somebody* was going to have to
pay for *that*.

The man wasn't done yet, though. He turned, took
a moment for his eyes to focus, and then charged at
Clint again. This time Clint met him with a kick that
caught him on the right knee. The man shouted out
in pain as his leg crumpled and fell to the floor.

By this time the first man had extricated himself
from Captain Bonet's hold. Bonet was lying on the
floor with his back to the wall as the first man
produced a knife from somewhere.

"Forget it," Clint said to him. The man turned and
Clint made as if to draw his gun. That froze the man
in place.

"Okay, take it easy," the man said. As an after-
thought he dropped the knife to the floor without
being told. "I'll just grab my friend and we'll be out
of here."

"Not before you answer a few questions, I'm
afraid," Clint said.

"Look, mister," the man said, "we thought the
room was empty and we were trying to rob it. That's
all."

"Forget it," Clint said. "I'm not buying that. Move
over there next to your friend."

The first man moved over and stood next to the
second man, who was still on the floor.

"Get up," Clint said to him.

"I can't," the man said. "I think you busted my
knee. Jesus, it hurts!"

"I'll save my sympathy for someone who needs

it," Clint said. "You fellas ready to answer some questions?"

"Yeah, yeah . . ." the first man said. "Go ahead and ask."

"You work for Cole Aldridge," Clint said. "He sent you over to grab Captain Bonet and either kidnap him or hurt him. Am I right?"

"Cole Aldridge?" the second man said. "We weren't hired by Aldridge." He was still holding his right knee, grimacing in pain.

Clint looked at Bonet, who shrugged.

"But you *were* hired to snatch the captain, right?" Clint asked.

The man's shoulders sagged and he said, "Yeah, that's right."

"All right," Clint said. "Then the man who hired you works for Aldridge. Who is he?"

The man on the floor exchanged looks with the first man and Clint said, "You fellas want to spend some time in jail for kidnapping?"

"All right, all right," the second man said, "but we weren't hired by a man. We were hired by a woman."

"A woman!" Bonet said in surprise.

"A woman," Clint said, shaking his head. There were only two possibilities here, and he didn't like either one of them.

He reached out and helped Bonet back to his feet. The captain took up a position right alongside Clint and glared at his two would-be kidnappers.

"All right," Clint said, "what's her name?"

THIRTY-EIGHT

Clint left Bonet in the care of J. P. Moses and his men and went to find the woman who worked for Cole Aldridge, and had been working for him all along. He found her in her room at her hotel.

"Those two fools I hired failed, huh?" she asked Clint when she opened her door and saw him standing there.

"I'm afraid so," Clint said.

"Too bad," she said. "I thought I could make this last a little longer."

"Why, Carla?" Clint asked Carla Dunlop. "Has the gambling stopped being enough for you?"

She shrugged and backed away so he could enter the room.

"In order to gamble the way you want to, Clint— the way *I* want to anyway—you have to have money behind you," Carla explained.

"And Aldridge offered you that money?"

She nodded, her eyes widening, and said, "Oh, lots of it—and he could afford it. If he could force Moses off the Mississippi this river would be a gold mine for him. I couldn't turn it down, and all I had to do for it was make sure that a few little accidents happened."

"Little accidents?" Clint said. "Like the winch breaking?"

"Sure, like that."

"A man got hurt, Carla."

"That was . . . unfortunate."

"I'm not buying this, Carla."

"What do you mean?"

"You weren't in on this alone," he said.

"Sure I was," she said, but her eyes were looking anywhere but at him.

"No," he said, with conviction, "you weren't. Oh, you could have hired those thugs to take out a couple of Moses' men, but the reason for that was to put a man of your own inside. You never could have taken care of that winch yourself. You had help. Who was it?"

For a moment he thought she was going to refuse to name her accomplice, but she obviously realized that the game was over.

"I didn't have to hire someone," she said. "He was already in place."

Clint knew that would bother Moses more than anything else, that the guilty party would turn out to be someone he had trusted.

"So then all you had to do was offer him some of Aldridge's money?"

"Money," she said, with a flirtatious smile, "and a little something else."

He ignored the comment, *and* the smile.

"Who was it?"

"His name is Grant," she said, "Al Grant."

"Grant?" Clint said, the disappointment plain in his voice.

"You didn't think it was him, huh?"

"No," he said, honestly. "I didn't think he'd turn against Moses for money."

"Well," she said, "it wasn't really the money that pushed him over the edge."

"It was that something else, eh?"

She shrugged.

"Well, I've sampled that something else myself," he said. "I guess I can understand how you could turn a man against his friends."

"Why, Clint?" she asked, starting to move towards him. "Is that a compliment?"

"It may have come out that way," he said, heading for the door, "but it wasn't meant that way."

THIRTY-NINE

J. P. Moses was even more disappointed than Clint was.

"Al?"

"I'm afraid so," Clint said.

"Maybe she was lying to you."

"I've already confronted him with it, Jack," Clint said.

"Where is he?"

"He's gone."

"You let him go?"

Clint nodded. "Her too," he added. "They were only working for Aldridge, and you're going to take care of him later today, in the race."

"I guess you're right," Moses said, shaking his head. "Carla and Al, huh?"

"Carla was the brains," Clint said, "and Al the brawn."

"I guess I can see how she'd turn a man's head, huh?" Moses said.

"That's what I said."

"Well," Moses said, "at least this means the race will be on the level—and Aldridge will never be able to beat us fair and square."

They were in the hotel dining room, having something to eat before the race.

"Well, it's time," Moses said.

They stood up and started out of the dining room into the lobby, where there was some commotion going on. Clint saw the red hair before he saw her face, and when he recognized Kelly he saw that she was being held by the wrist by a burly man in a suit.

"What's going on?" he said, stepping in front of the man and Kelly.

"Clint," Kelly said. He found it odd that instead of looking afraid, she looked embarrassed.

"You know this woman?" the man asked.

"I do," Clint said, "what's going on?"

"I'm the hotel detective, sir," the man said, "and I caught her coming out of someone's room with property that was not hers."

"What?" Clint looked at Kelly, who was now looking sheepish. "Kelly?"

She shrugged and said, "What can I say, Clint?"

"So you were the sneak thief on board the *Chance*?" he asked her.

"One of them. Someone else was working too. One of the passengers, I think." She paused. "I'm sorry," she said to Clint, then looked past him to Moses. "I'm sorry, Mr. Moses."

"Where are you taking her?" Moses asked the hotel detective.

"Over to the police station," the detective said.

"She works for me," Moses said. "I'll be over there soon to see what we can do about this."

"You'll have to talk to the police," the detective said, "and to the management of the hotel, sir. It will be up to them what's done. I have nothing to do with that. I just catch them."

"Mr. Moses—" Kelly Preston started, but Moses cut her off.

"Don't say anything now, Kelly," Moses said, "or I might change my mind. Maybe a night—or even a few days—in jail will do you some good."

She opened her mouth to say something, but the detective pulled her away and headed for the door with her.

"You're going to help her?" Clint asked.

"What can I do?" Moses said. "She's the best dealer I ever had—and she's my biggest draw."

Clint shook his head, and then walked over to the front desk.

"What room was she caught coming out of?" he asked the clerk.

"I believe it was one-oh-five, sir," the desk clerk replied.

Clint frowned, looked at Moses, and then said, "Shit, that's *my* room."

FORTY

From the hotel Moses went directly to the dock where Captain Bonet and their crew were waiting for him on *The Dead Man's Chance*. Clint Adams had not accompanied him, saying he had something else to do.

The dock was crowded with people, and Moses knew that all along the route, wherever possible, there would be people alongside the river, on both sides, cheering them on. Most of them wouldn't even care who won. A riverboat race was a great event *because* it was an event, not because anyone other than the principals involved cared who won.

Moses, standing just outside the wheelhouse, could see Cole Aldridge standing just outside the wheelhouse of *The Mississippi Palace*. He knew that Aldridge couldn't know that Carla and Al Grant had been found out. The man probably *still* felt like he had an ace in the hole. Moses couldn't wait until the race was over, when Aldridge would check that ace and find out that it was nothing but a joker.

"Got you," Moses said to Aldridge, even though the man couldn't hear him.

"Here comes Mr. Adams!" a crewman shouted up.

Moses changed sides, so he could look down at the dock instead of across the river at his opponent.

Clint was coming up the gangplank, carrying all of his gear. Obviously, he had cleaned out his room at the hotel. Maybe he didn't want to take the chance of something being stolen by *another* thief.

Moses stuck his head in the wheelhouse and said, "Get ready, Jacques. We'll be getting under way any time now."

"I'm ready, Boss," Bonet said, and then tapped the wheel and said, "And so is she. We'll show that other boat our heels."

Moses went down to intercept Clint on his way to his cabin.

"What's this?" he asked, indicating Clint's gear. "Does this mean you won't be coming back to New Orleans with us after the race?"

"That's what it means."

"But why? We'll be picking up all of our passengers, plus more. There'll be plenty of gambling—"

"I've had enough riverboat gambling for a while, Jack," Clint said.

"Well, then, what about New Orleans? It's a beautiful city."

"I know," Clint said. "But with Carla gone and Kelly in jail, there's not much reason for me to come back here after the race. I might as well *stay* in Natchez!"

Watch for

TWO GUNS FOR JUSTICE

133rd novel in the exciting GUNSMITH series
from Jove

Coming in January!

J.R. ROBERTS
THE
GUNSMITH